Mia measures up

SIMON SPOTLIGHT

An imprint of Simon & Schuster Children's Publishing Division

1230 Avenue of the Americas, New York, New York 10020

First Simon Spotlight paperback edition May 2017

Copyright © 2017 by Simon & Schuster, Inc.

All rights reserved, including the right of reproduction in whole or in part in any form.

SIMON SPOTLIGHT and colophon are registered trademarks of Simon & Schuster, Inc.

Text by Tracey West

Design and chapter header illustrations by Laura Roode

For information about special discounts for bulk purchases, please contact Simon & Schuster Special Sales at 1-866-506-1949 or business@simonandschuster.com.

Manufactured in the United States of America 0417 OFF

2 4 6 8 10 9 7 5 3 1

ISBN 978-1-4814-7903-5 (pbk)

ISBN 978-1-4814-7904-2 (hc)

ISBN 978-1-4814-7905-9 (eBook)

Library of Congress Catalog Card Number 2017934855

CUPCAKE DIARIES

Mia measures up

by coco simon

Simon Spotlight

New York   London   Toronto   Sydney   New Delhi

CHAPTER 1

Life Happens!

I shouldn't have eaten that third corn dog," my friend Katie Brown moaned. We were strapped inside a round blue chair on an amusement park ride, and we just kept spinning . . . spinning . . . and spinning. . . .

I looked over at her. Her brown ponytail was whipping back and forth, and her skin looked positively green. (Although that may have been caused by the flashing lights on the ride.)

"Don't puke on me! I just got these sneakers!" I warned her, laughing, and I saw Katie's knuckles tightly grip the bar in front of us.

"Don't say that word!" Katie yelled.

Luckily for both of us, the ride slowed to a stop. Katie and I climbed off. My legs felt wobbly.

"That was a close one," Katie said, leaning against a tree. "Whew!"

I looked at my phone. "It's almost five. We should get back to the table."

Katie nodded. "Right."

It was a beautiful twilight, and Katie and I were with our friends Alexis Becker and Emma Taylor at the Maple Grove Carnival. The four of us own a business together, the Cupcake Club. A few weeks ago Alexis had submitted a vendor application to the carnival so we could sell our cupcakes there, and they'd accepted us!

"I like that we're taking shifts," Katie said as we walked past a bouncy house with little kids going crazy inside. "I'm glad I had a chance to go on the rides."

"Even the Whirling Twirler?" I asked.

"Yes," Katie insisted. "In fact, I could go for another corn dog about now." She started looking around.

"Absolutely not!" I said. I grabbed her by the arm and started running toward our cupcake booth.

"But I love corn dogs!" Katie yelled behind me. "I would marry one if I could!"

We were both laughing so hard that I bumped right into someone. Luckily, it was someone we knew from school—George Martinez.

"Hey! The bumper cars are over there," George said, pointing.

"Sorry," I said.

Katie bumped into him too. "My turn!"

"Ouch! You're jabbing me with your pointy elbows!" George teased.

Katie and George are friends—the kind of friends who would be boyfriend and girlfriend if they were old enough to go on dates. So they're not boyfriend and girlfriend, but they do hang out together sometimes.

"Anyway, I'm doing serious business here," George said, nodding to the booth in front of us. "I need to buy my ticket to win the tickets to the La Vida Pasa concert before they do the drawing."

I nodded. "I bought mine earlier! So you might as well not bother buying your ticket, because I'm going to win."

"Wait, La Vida Pasa?" Katie asked. "What does that mean? 'Life passes'?"

"More like the saying, 'life happens,'" I replied. "Come on, you've heard me play them before. They're so good!"

"Oh yeah," Katie said. "They sing all in Spanish, right?"

3

"*Sí, amiga,*" George answered. "And they are *muy bueno.*"

He pulled some cash out of his pocket. "And now, if you'll excuse me, I need to buy the *winning* ticket."

"And we'd better get back to the table," Katie said.

"Good luck!" I called to George as we left. "You're going to need it."

Normally, I'm not a person who teases, but George teases everybody all the time (well, mostly Katie), so I thought I should dish it back to him for once.

Our little booth wasn't far away. My stepdad, Eddie, had set up a tent for us, and the park had provided everyone with tables. Ours had a pink tablecloth with our cupcake logo on the front.

Emma was handing a cupcake to a customer, and Alexis was putting change into our cashbox.

"How are we doing?" Katie asked after the customer had walked away.

"We sold sixteen more while you were gone!" Emma announced. "I think we'll sell out before this ends at six."

"We'll sell the last hour, if you two want to go do the rides," I said.

4

Emma looked at Alexis, and they both nodded.

"Whatever you do, don't eat three corn dogs before you go on the Whirling Twirler," Katie warned them.

Alexis's green eyes got wide. "Did you really do that?"

"Not my smartest decision," Katie replied.

"Well, I was thinking of getting a funnel cake," Emma said. "But maybe I'll do that after the rides."

"Mmmm, funnel cake," Katie said, and then she put her arms out in front of her and started to zombie-walk toward the funnel cake stand.

Once again, I grabbed her. "You're not going anywhere," I said. I took a look at the table. "We've got two dozen cupcakes left to sell."

"We sold out of the vanilla with rainbow sprinkles," Alexis reported. "But we always do. We need to push the maple walnut ones."

"Those are the best ones!" Katie said. "Maple walnut cupcakes for the Maple Grove Carnival. People need to be more adventurous with their cupcake choices."

"Hey, it's the Cupcake Sisters!"

We turned to see my cousin Sebastian and my stepbrother, Dan. Sebastian was the one who had called us the Cupcake Sisters.

"We're the Cupcake Club, not Cupcake Sisters," I told him.

"But you look like sisters," he said.

I shook my head. Katie, Alexis, Emma, and I don't look anything alike. I've got stick-straight black hair and dark brown eyes. Katie's got wavy, light brown hair that matches her eyes. Emma is blond haired and blue eyed, and Alexis is a green-eyed redhead.

"Just because we're all wearing the same T-shirt and we all have our hair in ponytails doesn't mean we look like sisters," I said.

Sebastian shrugged. "It's just my opinion."

"Yeah, he's, um, entitled to his opinion," Emma said awkwardly, and then she blushed a little bit.

"Come on, Emma. Let's get to the rides before they close," Alexis said, stepping out from behind the table. "We'll be back at six to help clean up!"

Katie and I got behind the table, and Dan reached for a chocolate cupcake.

"That'll be three dollars," I said.

"Really?" Dan asked. "I used to be your official cupcake taster, remember? Doesn't that count for something?"

"These cupcakes have already passed the taste test," I said. "Besides, you've got all that sweet pizza

6

delivery money. You can afford a cupcake."

Dan rolled his eyes and fished in his pocket for the cash. Katie took it from him.

"What about me?" asked Sebastian. "I'm too young to deliver pizza."

Sebastian is a freshman in high school, and Dan is a senior. Sebastian moved here a little while ago from Puerto Rico, and he and Dan bonded over heavy metal music, so they hang out all the time now.

Dan handed Katie another three dollars. "One more cupcake, please."

"Get the maple walnut," Katie said. "It's the best one."

Sebastian smiled. "Sure." He picked one up and bit into it. "Yeah, that's good."

Then Dan and Sebastian walked off, and Katie started hawking our cupcakes.

"Homemade cupcakes here! Get your maple walnut cupcakes!" she yelled.

A couple came over right away, and each of them bought a maple walnut cupcake.

"Keep going, Katie. It's working," I told her.

Katie moved to the front of the table. "Get your cupcakes here!" she sang, and then she busted out some crazy dance moves.

"Katie, what are you doing?" I asked.

"This is my happy cupcake dance!" she replied.

At that moment a group of girls walked past our booth. To be more specific they were the girls in the BFC (the Best Friends Club): Callie Wilson, Maggie Rodriguez, Olivia Allen, and Bella Kovacs.

"Nice dance, Katie," Olivia said in the most sarcastic voice possible, and the other girls giggled.

"Thank you!" Katie replied, still dancing. Most of us had learned to just ignore the behavior of the Best Friends Club.

Callie broke away from the others. "I'll have a chocolate cupcake, please," she said.

Now, maybe Callie just wanted a cupcake. Or maybe she did it because she and Katie used to be best friends before middle school, and I know that Callie feels bad when the other BFC girls are mean to Katie. Either way, it was nice of her.

I handed Callie her chocolate cupcake and then checked my phone.

"It's almost five thirty," I told Katie. "They're going to announce the winner of the concert tickets. I'm just going to get closer to the stage so I can hear, okay?"

Katie nodded. "Sure, I'll be fine."

I quickly made my way to the stage area, where all the announcements had been made throughout the day. It was almost dark now, and the park lights were shining. I got to the stage just as some members of the high school music club were getting to the microphone. I quickly took my ticket out of my pocket.

"We'd like to thank everyone who purchased a raffle ticket today. All proceeds are going to the music club," a girl was saying.

Then a boy picked a ticket out of a bag. "And the winner is . . . ticket 306978."

I stared at the ticket in my hand: 306978. The numbers were right there in front of me. I couldn't believe it. I'd won!

I ran up to the stage. "I think I have the winning ticket," I said, handing it to the girl. I still couldn't believe it was true.

She and the boy checked the numbers. Then the boy handed me a white envelope.

"Congratulations! You've won two tickets to see La Vida Pasa!"

I held back a scream of joy. "Thank you!"

As I raced back to tell Katie the good news, I passed George. He gave me the evil eye, but I knew he was only kidding.

"Sorry, George. Life happens," I told him, and then I ran back to the cupcake booth. I couldn't wait to tell Katie.

"Katie! I won! I won the tickets!" I yelled, waving the envelope.

Katie started jumping up and down. "Woo-hoo! Good for you!"

"You're coming with me, right?" I asked.

"Well, sure, yeah," she said. "But I don't really know their music."

"It's great!" I said. "We'll have fun."

"And I won't really understand the words," Katie went on.

"That's okay," I said. "You know my Spanish is terrible. I used to think one of their songs was about a lost dog, but it's really about a lost love."

Katie laughed. "All right, I'll go. Thanks—it's nice of you to give me the ticket. When is it?"

"Three weeks from now, on a Friday," I replied. "This is going to be awesome."

"*Sí!*" Katie agreed.

CHAPTER 2

Too Young? Seriously?

Thanks to Katie's yelling and dancing, we sold out of our cupcakes just before the carnival ended at six o'clock. Alexis and Emma came back to the table so we could pack up, and Eddie arrived to help us take down the tent.

"Any leftovers for me?" Eddie asked when he arrived.

"No, Mr. Valdes. We sold out," Alexis replied.

"Rats!" Eddie said. "I wanted to buy some of your maple walnut ones."

As he said it, Eddie rubbed his belly, which had gotten a little bigger since my friends and I had started our Cupcake business. He was our best customer. I think part of the reason is that he likes cupcakes, but mostly, it's because he likes to support us.

I got lucky after my parents divorced. Not because they got divorced—that was really sad—but because my mom married Eddie, who is just about the nicest stepdad ever. And my real dad stayed in the picture. He still lives in Manhattan, where I grew up, and I visit with him every other weekend, and half of every summer.

We packed up our empty cupcake carriers and business flyers. Then we all helped to take down the tent, and I said good-bye to my friends and helped Eddie carry it to the car.

"I hope you didn't eat too much junk food at the carnival," Eddie said as we drove home. "Your mom is making her spicy shrimp tonight. The house smells amazing."

"I didn't, but Katie did," I said, and I told him the corn dog story. Eddie laughed.

"How does that girl stay so skinny?" he wondered.

"I think it's all the running she does in track," I replied.

We pulled into the driveway, and Dan's car was there.

"Good, Dan and Sebastian are here," he said. "We can eat right away."

I wasn't surprised to hear that Sebastian was

eating dinner with us. Ever since he'd moved to New Jersey, he was at our house a lot, and not just because he and Dan had formed a band. His mom, my aunt Laura—technically, she's my second or third cousin or something, but I call her Aunt Laura—works as a nurse in the city, and her hours are crazy. So Sebastian has become almost like a second brother.

I stepped inside the house, and Eddie was right—it smelled great. My two little white dogs, Tiki and Milkshake, ran up to greet me.

"Wash your hands, Mia; we're going to eat!" Mom called from the kitchen.

"Okay!" I called back, and I gave each dog a scratch on the head before heading to the powder room to wash up.

Then I took my seat in our dining room, my usual seat next to Mom. Dan and Sebastian sat across from us, and Eddie sat at the head of the table. There was a big platter of Mom's spicy shrimp in tomato sauce in the middle of the table, along with a bowl of rice and peas and another bowl of salad.

"So how was the carnival?" Mom asked as she sat down.

Dan was shoveling food into his mouth and

didn't answer. Everyone stared at him until finally Sebastian spoke up.

"It was fun," said Sebastian. "I wish there was more music playing, though."

"Speaking of music, I have an announcement," I said. "I won two tickets to La Vida Pasa!"

"Hey! Lucky Mia!" Eddie congratulated me.

Dan put down his fork. "You won those? No way."

"We wanted to win," said Sebastian.

"Wait a second, you guys want to see La Vida Pasa?" I asked. "They're not a heavy metal band. They're, like, the complete opposite of heavy metal."

"So what? They're awesome," Dan said.

"And they're huge in Puerto Rico," responded Sebastian. "I was so excited when I saw they were playing here in New Jersey. You have to take me with you!"

"I've already told Katie I'm taking her," I said.

Mom looked at me. "And where, exactly, is this concert?" she asked.

"At the Rockwood Arts Center," I replied. "It's not far. You can drive us, right? And then pick us up when it's over?"

I was not prepared for Mom's response.

"Absolutely not," she said. "Mia, you are too young to go to a concert by yourself."

"But I'll be with Katie," I said.

"You know what I mean," Mom said. "It's at night, and it will be crowded, and you need an adult to go with you."

I looked at Eddie. A lot of times he is less strict than Mom. But he stopped me before I could even appeal to him.

"Your mother is right, Mia," he said. "You're too young to do something like this on your own."

I stood up. "Are you serious?" I asked, and I knew I was getting loud. "I run a business with my friends. Every other weekend, I take a train to Manhattan all by myself. So why am I too young for a concert?"

"Mia, sit down," Mom said in her no-nonsense voice. "Don't you think I get nervous sending you on that train all by yourself? The only reason I let you do it is because I know your father will be there at Penn Station, waiting for you. This is different."

I plopped back down onto my seat. I felt like crying. "So you're saying I can't go to the concert?"

"I'll go with you," Eddie offered.

I groaned. I like Eddie a lot, but I did not want to go with him see a pop band full of cute boys.

"Hey, I have an idea," Sebastian said. "What if

Dan and I go with you? You can give us your extra ticket, and we'll split the cost of the third ticket to be fair."

"Or she could give *me* her free ticket because I'm her stepbrother," Dan said.

"And I'm her cousin, and it was my idea," Sebastian said.

"That's actually a good solution, Sebastian," Mom said, and I was astounded.

"I thought you said I had to go with an adult? Dan's not an adult," I pointed out.

"He's close enough," Mom said. "Or would you rather go with Eddie?"

"I would rather go with Katie," I said stubbornly. "I already promised her the extra ticket. I can't take it back now."

"Well, you shouldn't have done that without talking to me first," Mom said, and I stared down at my plate. Leave it to Mom to take something awesome and happy and ruin it!

"Cheer up, Mia. It will be fun," Sebastian said. "And Katie could always buy her own ticket if she really wants to go."

"That's not the same," I said, still refusing to look up. I pushed the food around on my plate with my fork.

"So, we're supposed to have another beautiful day tomorrow," Eddie said, changing the subject like he usually does when things get uncomfortable. "Maybe we can go for a little hike? How does that sound?"

Then everybody started talking, except for me, because I was still too upset. Too young! I still couldn't believe it. How could Mom let me go back and forth to Manhattan but not let me go to a concert? It made no sense.

After dinner I helped clear the table and load the dishwasher.

"Well, I guess I have to tell Katie she can't go to the concert with me," I said in a very loud voice, to make sure everyone heard me. But nobody said anything.

So I went up to my room and shut the door. Then I texted Katie: Bad news! My mom is being ridiculous and won't let me go to the concert with you without an adult. Have to take Dan and Sebastian.☹

That's okay, Katie texted back. I don't really know the group anyway, and you will have a good time with your bro and Sebastian.

That's what I like about Katie. She is chill about most things. I hardly ever have any drama with her.

Can you believe my mom said I'm too young? Makes no sense! I texted back.

It's a mom thing, Katie replied. I still can't stay in the house by myself after 9 p.m. If Mom goes out late with Jeff, I have to stay with you, or she makes Mrs. Wortham babysit me. Who always smells like cabbage.

I couldn't remember the last time I'd had a baby-sitter. If Mom and Eddie did late-night stuff, they usually did it on weekends when I was with my dad. Or else they would leave me here with Dan.

A terrible thought occurred to me. Was Dan my babysitter? I had never thought of it that way before, but now it was starting to make sense. Is that why they were okay with him going to the concert with me?

I let this sink in. Dan, who leaves his dirty socks all over the house and never remembers to feed Tiki and Milkshake when I have a Cupcake job. Mom thought Dan was more mature than me? So what if he was a senior in high school? Wasn't it a scientific fact that girls matured faster than boys? I would have to do some research on that.

But I knew deep down, if there were a maturity contest, me versus Dan, I would win!

Why didn't Mom understand that?

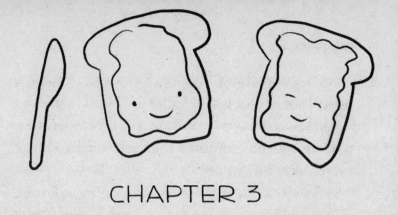

CHAPTER 3

Too Old for P-B-and-J?

𝒯he next day Mom dropped me off at Katie's house at five o'clock for a Cupcake Club meeting. When I got there, the front door was open.

"Come on in!" Katie called from inside.

I walked in and headed right to Katie's kitchen. It's a homey, comfortable room with a big pantry on the side that is perfect for holding baking supplies. Sometimes when the Cupcake Club meets, it's to bake a test batch of cupcakes or to bake the cupcakes we need for an event. But sometimes, like tonight, we meet to do business planning.

I would rather decorate cupcakes than talk about profit and loss, but Alexis loves that stuff, which is a good thing. Because of her, we actually make some money selling our cupcakes. And that is also a good thing because I'm saving up for a new pair of winter boots. I am convinced that some designer, somewhere, has made a pair of boots that stand up to snow and still look fashionable. But I haven't found them yet.

Anyway, Alexis and Emma were sitting at Katie's kitchen table. Katie was opening up two pizza boxes on the counter.

"The pizza just came!" she said. "Grab yourself a drink. There's water and sparkling apple cider."

I opted for the water (to make up for the cotton candy I'd had the day before), pouring it from a pitcher, and sat down next to Emma.

"What kind did you get?" I asked, nodding to the pizzas.

"Half plain for Alexis, half pepperoni for Emma, half tomato basil for you, and half broccoli for me," Katie said.

"Katie, you think of everything," Emma said.

Katie put a plate in front of each of us and handed me a jar of red pepper flakes before she sat down. Then she held up her glass of sparkling cider.

"Cheers!" she said, and we clinked glasses.

Emma took a bite of her pizza. "Mmm, this is good."

"Definitely," Alexis agreed, "but greasy. I had

some reports to give out, but I'll wait until the pizza's done."

"We can talk about the jobs we've got coming up," Katie suggested. "We need to come up with flavor ideas."

Alexis nodded, wiped her hands on a napkin, and picked up her phone. "Okay, in three weeks we've got the party for the Smiths and the party for the Maple Grove Senior Home on the same day."

"What's the date again?" Emma asked, and she checked her phone as Alexis told her. "I thought I had a modeling gig then, but it's the week after that. So I can help."

"That's the day after the La Vida Pasa concert," I said. "So I can't bake the night before. But I can help all day Saturday."

"Maybe the rest of us can bake Friday night, and then we can decorate together on Saturday morning," Alexis suggested. "We'll work that out. In the meantime we can figure out the flavors so we can get the shopping done."

"So, the Smith party is for little kids, right?" Katie asked.

Alexis nodded. "Evan is turning two, and Ella is four and Caleigh is six," she reported. "The party is for Evan's birthday, and there will be thirty little kids running around over there. Should be fun."

Katie shuddered. "Oh boy." Katie's good with kids, but she's an only child, so it kind of freaks her out to be around a lot of them. I was an only child too, until I got Dan as a stepbrother, but I'm okay with little kids, I guess—except when they're messy.

"We should keep the cupcakes simple," I said. "There's no point in making them look beautiful when those kids are just going to smear them everywhere."

"Is there a theme?" Emma asked.

Alexis looked at her phone. "I just wrote down 'blue and red,'" she replied.

"Ooh, we could do P-B-and-J cupcakes!" Katie cried. "We haven't done those in a while. And some could have blueberry jelly inside, and some could have strawberry."

"That's not a bad idea," Alexis said. "I'll need to check and make sure there are no peanut allergy concerns, though."

Katie frowned. "Oh yeah. That's a bummer."

I took a bite of my pizza, wishing I had my sketchbook in front of me. Ideas for designs were swirling around in my brain.

"Maybe we could do fun designs," I said. "You

know, red icing with blue polka dots. Or blue icing with red stars. Stuff like that."

"It's hard to get pure red icing," Katie said. "You need a lot of food coloring, and then the icing just tastes gross. Maybe stick with blue icing and use red gel to make the designs."

"Or red candies!" Emma said.

Katie nodded. "That would be awesome!"

Alexis wiped her hands on her napkin again. "Okay, forget the grease; I really need to be writing this down."

She went to her backpack and retrieved her Cupcake Club ledger that she uses to keep us organized. She also took out a small notebook, along with a pink pen with a little cupcake on top, and started to take notes.

"So, we'll do P-B-and-J cupcakes unless there's an issue," she said. "Could we do vanilla cake with the jelly if the peanut butter is out?"

"Sure," Katie replied.

Alexis continued writing. "Blue icing, red candy decorations." Then she looked up. "Okay, now we need to talk about the party at the senior home. Gladys Bailey is turning one hundred, and they're having a party for her."

"Maybe we could just make the P-B-and-J

cupcakes for that party too, to keep things simple," Katie said. "Just with a different icing or decorations."

Alexis frowned. "I don't think old people like peanut butter and jelly."

"Why not?" Katie challenged.

Alexis shrugged. "I don't know. That just feels like a kid flavor to me."

Emma nodded. "I think Alexis is on to something. My parents never bring P–B–and–J to work for lunch. It's always, like, a salad or Thai noodles or something like that."

Katie shook her head. "I don't get it. Why does something like peanut butter have to be only for kids? It's delicious!"

"Well, it's delicious, but maybe it's not sophisticated enough," I said.

"And how do we know if Gladys Bailey is sophisticated or not?" Katie asked. "Maybe she loves peanut butter and watches cartoons and stuff like that."

"Why don't you ask her?" Alexis suggested.

"I will!" Katie said. "The senior home is close to the school. I'll go there and find out what she likes."

"Wait, what if the party is going to be a surprise?" Emma asked. "We don't want to spoil it."

I grinned. "Something tells me they wouldn't have a surprise party for a one-hundred-year-old person. I don't think it would be a good idea to yell 'surprise' at someone who is a hundred! But that's just a guess."

"Yeah, the shock might be too much," Katie said.

"I will call the Maple Grove Senior Home and find out if it's a surprise party," Alexis said. "Then, Katie, if you want to go there and talk to Gladys, go right ahead. But do it soon. The party *is* in three weeks."

Katie nodded. "I'm on it. And whatever happens, I vow that I will never stop liking P-B-and-J, not even if I live to one hundred!"

I sighed. "Maybe when I'm one hundred, my mom will finally let me do things on my own."

"What do you mean?" Emma asked.

"Well, you know I won those tickets to see La Vida Pasa, right?" I asked, and they nodded. "I had promised Katie that she could go with me, but Mom said no! Even though it's right here in New Jersey. She's making me take Dan and Sebastian. I almost had to go with Eddie!"

"Well, I don't think my mom would let me do that either," Alexis said. "Emma and I wanted to go see Twice Shy over the summer at an outdoor festival, and Mom went with us. It was so embarrassing!"

"It wasn't so bad," Emma said. "At least she kept her distance most of the time."

"But she was staring at us! I could feel her eyes on me the whole time!" Alexis remembered.

"Well, my mom might be loosening up a little bit, and she might start letting me stay home alone," Katie said. "But I still can't use the oven or even the microwave when she's not there."

"My parents are weird," Emma said. "They give me all this responsibility, like how I have to watch Jake and bring him to peewee soccer practices and stuff. But then they make me go to bed at ten on school nights! So I'm responsible enough to watch Jake but not responsible enough to go to bed when I want to? It makes no sense."

The kitchen was silent for a moment as we all thought about how unfair our lives were.

"It's going to get better in high school," Alexis declared. "Dylan gets to do whatever she wants."

"High school!" I groaned. "But that's, like, so far away."

"Yeah!" agreed Katie.

"Well, high school is pretty hard too," Emma

pointed out. "Sam always has a ton of homework, and he spends all his time on college applications. He's superstressed out."

"So what you're saying is, we can have no responsibilities and no freedom, or lots of responsibilities and lots of freedom?" Katie asked.

"I didn't think of it like that," Emma said, frowning. "You're thinking very negatively."

"But it's not balanced!" I argued. "Like you said, Emma, you have responsibilities already. We all do. Why do our parents keep saying we're too young to do stuff?"

Alexis looked at the clock. "I think we're all going to reach one hundred before this meeting is over. Let's clean up and look at those reports. We had record profits last month."

We all stood up to clear off the table. Even though I was with my friends and had just eaten delicious pizza, I was feeling pretty crabby.

It looked like I would have to wait until high school to be treated like a responsible adult. I didn't think I could wait that long!

CHAPTER 4

Dad Doesn't Get Fashion!

That next week went by pretty slowly because I was really looking forward to spending the weekend with my dad in Manhattan. When I'm with Dad and he has to go out someplace, he lets me stay in the apartment by myself. And he lets me and my friend Ava ride the subway together if we're going to a park or one of Ava's friend's apartments. I knew he wouldn't have a problem with me and Katie going to that concert.

I was ready to pour out the whole story that Friday night as we ate sushi in our favorite Japanese restaurant, Tokyo 16. But first I took a photo of my spicy tuna roll and posted it on PicPop. It's this new app that everyone in my school was using, where you post photos and people you're connected to can like and comment on them. It's supposed to be safe for kids because it's monitored for profanity and other stuff like that, so Mom let me sign up.

I posted the photo, and Katie liked it right away. I smiled and then launched into my story.

"So, she doesn't think I'm mature enough to be at that concert with Katie," I was telling him between bites of sushi. "But Dan is!"

"Well, he is almost five years older than you, sweetheart," Dad said.

I'm pretty sure I scowled. "But everyone knows that girls mature faster than boys. It's, like, a scientific fact."

I still wasn't sure about that, but I was pleased when Dad nodded. "You have a point there, *mija*, but you know the rules. I can't overturn your mother's decisions, especially when they have to do with what's happening in New Jersey."

I wasn't expecting that from Dad. "But you see my point, right?" I asked.

Dad looked uncomfortable. He called over our server. "Two more iced green teas, please."

"Sure, Mr. Cruz." The server was a pretty woman, and she gave my dad a big smile before she walked away. I wasn't surprised about that. My dad is a good-looking guy, I guess. He's tall with dark, curly hair and always dresses well. Tonight, he was wearing a black suit with a black dress shirt and tie underneath. He likes the monochromatic thing because he says it makes his life easier—but it also pretty much ensures that he always looks good.

"She knows your name?" I asked him.

"Oh, I've just been coming here a lot lately," Dad said with a little shrug. "You get to know people. Besides, Lisa's nice."

"Another girlfriend?" I asked cautiously. Dad has had a few different girlfriends since he and Mom divorced. I'm always happy when he breaks up with the bad ones, and I'm always a little sad when he breaks up with the good ones. It was like an emotional roller coaster!

"No," Dad said flatly. "The next time I get a girlfriend, you'll be the first to know. Okay?"

I thought about this. "Well . . . sure. Just feel free to go on a few dates first before you call someone your girlfriend. Weed out the weird ones before they get to me."

Dad laughed. "Maybe you're right about the maturity thing, Mia. That's pretty good advice."

I smiled. *One for Mia!* I thought.

"Any plans for tomorrow?" he asked me. "I've had a busy week. I hadn't planned anything for us."

"Well, to be honest, I have a lot of homework," I replied. "But I was hoping to get out and do some shopping. I need winter boots, and I've got Cupcake money saved up."

"She gives good advice *and* saves her money," Dad said. "I'm very proud of you, Mia. How about this: We'll get some brunch tomorrow and then go shopping. You can do your homework when we get back."

I nodded. "Great! Thanks! I know just the place I need to look for boots, and it isn't far from the apartment."

Dad's apartment is in downtown Manhattan. I have my own room there, and it's really nice. We decorated it with a Parisian chic theme. The walls are pale pink with black-and-white accents. My headboard is wrought iron, and my bedspread and pillows have a really nice black-and-white pattern on them. I have an adorable white vanity where I can keep all my hair stuff. The closet is really small, though, but that's okay because I keep most of my clothes in New Jersey and bring an overnight bag with me when I visit Dad.

That night we watched a movie together, and the next morning we set out for our brunch-shopping adventure. Once, Katie asked me if it was a pain to go back and forth from Manhattan to New Jersey every other week. I understand why it might look that way, but really, my Manhattan weekends are almost always magical. Dad loves to go out to eat, and between the museums and parks and shops, there's always so much to do. Besides that, my other best friend, Ava Monroe, lives here.

Ava was visiting her aunt in Queens that weekend, or normally, she would have come shopping with us. Dad and I had both slept a little late, and we got to a restaurant for brunch at eleven thirty. We both had the huevos rancheros—eggs with salsa, tortillas, and beans—and then we walked to Soul, my favorite shoe store in downtown Manhattan.

Usually, Soul would be out of my price range, but every once in a while they have a great sale, and this weekend was it. I was practically jumping up and down when Dad and I got to the store.

"Fifty percent off!" I cried, pointing to a sign. "And just *look* at all those boots!"

I raced to the boot display and took them all in. Black leather boots. Brown leather boots. Pleather boots in funky colors. Boots with spiked heels and chunky heels. Boots with fur trim. Boots with square toes and pointy toes.

And then I saw them: the boots of my dreams.

They were tall and black, with the cuffs rolled over at the tops, and button details. I picked them up. The bottoms were chunky rubber—perfect for slippery winter sidewalks.

I sat down to try them on, grateful I had worn a skirt and tights so I could try on the boots without my pant legs getting in the way. I slipped on the boots, and the leather felt so soft! They came up to just over my knees.

I checked them out in the mirror, and honestly, I looked fabulous! Then I walked up to Dad, who was checking out the men's dress shoes, and tapped him on the shoulder. "What do you think?"

Dad turned around. "No, Mia." He shook his head. "Those boots are not for someone your age. Take them off, please."

I was surprised. "Are you kidding? Over-the-knee boots are in!" I protested.

"Maybe they're in for actresses who go clubbing, but not for my daughter," Dad said.

I got angry. "Well, it's my money," I said. "I earned it."

Dad lowered his voice. "And as long as you live with your parents, we are going to have a say in what you do with that money," he said quietly but firmly.

I caught one of the saleswomen looking at us, so I went back to the bench without another word.

When I was sure Dad wasn't looking, I took a selfie of me in the boots and texted Mom. What do you think? Dad says too grown-up for me, but these are in style, right?

Mom texted back right away: He's right! No over-the-knee boots, Mia. Find something else.

I was really angry now. I texted Mom ☹ and then yanked off the boots.

The saleswoman came up to me. "Can I help you find something?"

She had a look of empathy on her face, and I liked her sense of style; sandy brown hair in two low-braided pigtails, a black lace dress over black leggings, and chunky boots.

"Yes, please," I said. "I'm looking for something black, and good for winter, but that doesn't look like a winter boot. And no over-the-knee boots." I motioned to the boots I'd just taken off.

She smiled and picked up the boots, looking at the size on the label. "Let me see what I can find for you. I'm Meg."

I started to feel a little better. Meg was really nice, and really patient, and she helped me try on six pairs of boots until I found the right pair. They weren't exactly what I had in mind, but they were nice. They went up to the middle of my calves and had a big buckle halfway up the boot. And the heel was low, chunky and sturdy but still fashionable.

Dad walked up to me as I was modeling the boots. "Much better."

"Well, not *much* better, but I like them," I said, still unwilling to admit that the other boots were not a good purchase.

"And they're fifty percent off," Meg reminded me with smile.

That cheered me up. "That's great. I still have some Cupcake money left." I looked over at the jewelry counter. "I could use some new earrings."

"How about I get the earrings for you, *mija*?" Dad asked.

"Wow, sure," I said. "Thanks!" Some people would say that my dad spoils me . . . and I would have to say that they're right.

While Meg packed up the boots, I looked over the earrings. There were tiny studs, and long dangly ones, but my eyes were drawn to a pair of big silver hoops. I had always wanted a pair like that. I reached for them.

"Okay?" I asked, showing them to Dad, and he nodded. I was relieved. For a second I was worried that he was going to say they were too grown-up!

We paid for my boots and earrings, and I thanked Meg. After we left the shop, we stopped at a coffee shop on the way home.

"A little fuel for your homework?" Dad asked, and I nodded, ordering an iced caramel latte with skim milk. Mom almost never lets me drink coffee at her house.

Two for Mia! I congratulated myself.

When we got back to the apartment, I decided to play dress up before starting my homework. I put on the new boots and slipped the big hoop earrings into my ears.

I looked in the mirror and frowned. I had put my hair in two high pigtails that morning. With the big hoop earrings, I looked like a little girl playing dress up!

I took out the elastics, letting my hair cascade down. That looked okay, but I didn't really get the full effect of the earrings. I tried a ponytail in the back, but then the earrings totally dominated my face.

Then I remembered Meg back at the shoe shop, and her two low braids. I quickly started braiding my hair and then stepped back to look.

The braids were a little messy, but I could work

on that. But the hair looked fantastic on me! And it looked especially great with the earrings.

"I am definitely going to try out this look on Monday morning," I told my reflection in the mirror. "So I guess that's three for Mia!"

I didn't know it then, but those low-braided pigtails were going to cause me major drama!

CHAPTER 5

Who Is Sarrah Sleepz?

I didn't groan Monday morning when the alarm went off because I was excited to try out my new look. First, I checked the weather app. It was going to be unseasonably cold—in the low fifties—which meant that it was perfect weather to wear my new boots.

I pulled on my blue pleated short skirt over my black tights and topped it with my favorite black sweater with a blue camisole underneath. Then I braided my hair in the low pigtails I had practiced the day before. Finally, I added the big hoop earrings.

I toyed with the idea of adding a silver necklace, but honestly, the earrings were a big enough statement that I decided against it. My mom is a professional stylist, and she's taught me a lot about editing my look. It's easy to go overboard with jewelry, scarves, and other accessories.

"Coco Chanel said that simplicity is the key to all elegance," Mom would always say, "and she was right."

And anyway, I looked great. Perfect, even. I picked up my phone and made my best selfie face—the one where I smile with my eyes, not my mouth. (It takes practice, but when you get it right, it's amazing!) I took a few selfies and then posted the best one on PicPop.

I went downstairs and took a yogurt out of the refrigerator. Dan was eating a huge pile of waffles, and Mom and Eddie were drinking their coffee and eating toast.

I had just started eating my yogurt when my phone made a sound.

Pop!

"What was that?" Eddie asked.

I picked up my phone. "It's the sound you get when someone likes your photo on PicPop."

Pop! Pop!

"Wow, you must have posted a good photo," Eddie said.

"Is that the app I let you join?" Mom asked, and

I nodded. "Let me see the photo, please."

I handed over the phone with a sigh. "Do you really think I would post something inappropriate? The site won't allow that, anyway. It's perfectly safe."

Mom looked at the picture. "That's lovely, Mia," she said. She handed the phone back to me, ignoring my comment.

Pop! Pop!

Dan rolled his eyes.

"What's your problem?" I asked him.

"I hear that sound all day long in school," he said. "It gets on your nerves. Why do you need people you don't even know to like pictures of you? It's dumb."

"They're not people I don't know; they're my friends," I countered. "And it's a way to share things and support one another."

"How about you two support each other and finish this argument?" Eddie asked. "You're going to be late for school."

I quickly finished my yogurt, brushed my teeth, put on a jacket, and headed for the bus stop. I climbed on the bus, and after the first stop, Katie got on.

"Whoa, cool earrings," she said. "You could throw a basketball through those."

"Thanks," I said, because I knew Katie meant that as a compliment.

"How was your weekend?" Katie asked.

"Good," I replied. "I got these earrings. And these boots." I lifted up my feet.

"Nice!" Katie said. "So, guess what I did? I met Gladys Bailey!"

I looked at her, puzzled.

"The lady who's going to turn one hundred," Katie reminded me. "I went to the nursing home and met the activities director, and she said that Gladys knew about the party and that I could meet her."

"What was she like?" I asked.

"Really nice," Katie replied. "She's got this white hair that looks just like cotton candy. She used to be a newspaper reporter and lived in Manhattan, but her daughter moved her out here when she turned eighty, and she's been here ever since."

"She must miss Manhattan," I said. I know I would miss it if I didn't get to go back every other week.

Katie nodded. "She does. So I'm thinking maybe we could do New York City–themed cupcakes."

A dozen ideas popped into my head right away. "That will be so cool! What about the flavor, though? Do you know her preferences?"

"Well, she does like peanut butter, so I was right about that," Katie said. "But it's not her favorite. She says her favorite flavor is cream soda!"

"Cream soda?" I asked.

Katie shook her head. "I know. I mean, how do you get a cupcake to taste like cream soda? But I've already started researching. I'll make it work."

"And I'll figure out the decorations," I promised.

The bus pulled up at the school, and then Monday kicked in. Normally, I am not a fan of Mondays, but this one went pretty smoothly. On my way to first period, I passed my friends Lucy Moss and Sophie Baudin in the hallway.

"Wow, love your hair today, Mia," Lucy said.

"Yeah, love your hair," Sophie echoed.

"Thanks," I replied. "Just trying something new."

Pop! I heard my photo get another like—which reminded me that I needed to turn off my phone or risk getting it confiscated. I switched it off and didn't think about it until the end of the day.

After school I turned my cell back on and quickly checked the pic—seventy-three likes! I saw there were a bunch of comments, but I had a big history test to study for. When I got home,

I stayed in my room until dinnertime, studying. Mrs. Kratzer's tests are tough, and she really picks apart our essay question answers.

Eddie made meat loaf and mashed potatoes for dinner, and Sebastian came over to eat with us, as usual. So I wasn't too surprised when the doorbell rang as we were clearing the table, and it turned out to be Emma.

"Hey," I said. "Did you um, come to see . . ." I nodded behind me toward Sebastian. I knew she had kind of a crush on him.

"No!" Emma said, and her cheeks turned pink. "Actually, I need to talk to you, Mia. It's important."

Emma looked really upset, and I suddenly felt worried. "Sure, come upstairs."

A minute later we were in my room, with the door closed, sitting on my bed.

"What's wrong?" I asked.

Emma handed me her phone. "So, this girl I friended on PicPop posted your selfie from this morning."

"So?" I asked.

"Just read it," Emma said.

I looked at the comment by the girl who had reposted my selfie—someone named Sarrah Sleepz.

Nice braids, Pippi Longstocking.

I took this in. "Okay, not the nicest comment in the world. But at least she used a literary reference."

"There's more," Emma said. "Keep scrolling."

LOL! Fashion backward!
Does she think she's in Frozen or something?
It's a hair-don't!
And those earrings! Major fail!

All these comments were from people I didn't know. Then Sarrah Sleepz chimed in again.

Guess Mighty Mia isn't all that.

Then I saw someone I knew—Starr123, otherwise known as Olivia Allen.

Mia has never been all that! She's a loser, and this proves it.

"Ouch," I said. "This is pretty harsh."

Emma nodded. "I know. I thought you should see it. They're just being stupid."

"Haters gonna hate," I said. Normally, I try to not let stuff like this bother me. I like to do my own thing, and sometimes other people don't like it. The way I see it, that's their deal, not mine.

Still, I was used to people saying stuff to my face. This felt like a sneak attack or something.

"Who is this Sarrah Sleepz, and how did she get my photo to repost it?" I wondered out loud.

"She might have seen it when I liked your photo and then copied it to her phone," Emma said.

"You mean, anyone who sees a photo I post can copy it?" I asked.

"Unless you post all your photos as pals only," Emma replied. "But then you won't get as many likes, so nobody ever does that."

I frowned and started scrolling through my PicPop pals list. There she was, Sarrah Sleepz! In her profile photo, she had her head under the covers of her bed so you couldn't see her face. I scrolled through her other photos, but there were no photos of her face anywhere! Weird. Then I checked her pals list.

"Wait, it looks like *I* friended Sarrah Sleepz!" I said, surprising myself. "She's friends with Callie, so I must have figured that she's someone from our school just using a silly name."

"You can block her," Emma suggested.

"Doing that now," I said, quickly typing on my phone. "I'm setting my photos to 'pals only,' too."

"Good idea," Emma said. "That's what I do."

I put down my phone and gave her a hug. "Thanks! You saved me."

Emma smiled. "That's what friends are for."

We came downstairs to find Mom waiting for us. "Emma, I thought I heard you. What were you girls doing?"

"Just talking," Emma said. "I, um, had a problem, and Mia helped me out."

Eddie walked up. "I have a problem. I baked cookies, and I need someone to help me eat them. Can you stay for cookies?"

"Yeah, come eat some cookies, chicas!" Sebastian yelled from the kitchen.

I looked at Emma and smiled. "I'm sure Emma would love to."

"Of course I would," Emma said, and her cheeks turned pink again.

So we went into the kitchen and ate cookies with everybody, and Sebastian did a funny impression of his teacher that made everyone laugh.

And I was sort of laughing too, but inside, I kept thinking the same thing over and over: Who was Sarrah Sleepz? And why was she calling me out?

CHAPTER 6

Mom Flips Out!

On Tuesday I didn't post anything on PicPop, just to be safe. I kept checking my page, and nothing popped up from Sarrah Sleepz (because I blocked her), and I didn't see anybody who was pals with Sarrah Sleepz popping about me. ("Popping" in PicPop means when you comment.)

And I kept my hair in the braids. I liked them, and they were easy to do in the morning.

On Wednesday it was chilly enough outside for me to wear a scarf around my neck. Not the winter scarf kind. This was a pretty blue scarf with tiny pom-poms on it that my aunt had given me for my birthday. I tied it on over my scoop-necked top, and it looked great. I couldn't resist, so I took a selfie and posted it.

Pop! Pop! Pop! The sound of people liking my photo followed me down the stairs. I had to admit, it was kind of an addictive feeling. The more pops I heard, the more I knew that I had posted a cute picture.

When I checked my phone again after school, eighty-three people had liked my photo, and I felt pretty good. I was glad the whole Sarrah Sleepz thing was over.

Or so I thought.

Katie, Alexis, and Emma all came home with me after school for a test baking session. We do those sometimes when we want to try a new flavor. It's a bad idea to try out something new the day of your cupcake event, because if something goes wrong, or it doesn't taste good, there's no time to fix it.

"So are we really making cream soda cupcakes?" Emma asked as my friends and I deposited our backpacks in the little shoe room attached to the kitchen. (Eddie calls it a "mudroom," but that has always sounded gross to me!)

Katie nodded. "It's Gladys's favorite flavor, and she asked for it. I looked online, and there are a few recipes for how to do it. Usually, the cream soda goes in the batter, and then the frosting is vanilla or brown butter or something like that, to pump up the cream soda flavor."

"Mmm, sounds yummy," Emma said.

I picked up the shopping bag on the counter and pulled out a bottle of cream soda.

"Mom found this for us at the health food store," I said. "It's made from natural ingredients by, like, cream soda experts or something. It's supposed to be really good."

"Nothing but the finest for Gladys!" Katie said. "If it's okay with you guys, I'll start on the batter. I need to experiment a little bit with the cream soda ratio."

"Do you have a frosting recipe? We can start on that," Alexis said.

Katie handed Alexis an index card. "Got it right here."

"And I still need to figure out the decorations," I said. I took out my phone. "I found this one blogger who's done really cute fondant decorations with a New York City theme."

Pop! My phone made the PicPop noise again. Alexis looked up.

"You know, we haven't talked about that cyberbully who targeted you," she said.

"Cyberbully." "Targeted." That sounded harsh!

"It wasn't a big deal," I said with a shrug.

"But I don't like the idea that Sarrah Sleepz is using a fake identity to get to you," Alexis said. "We should get to the bottom of who she is."

"It's fine," I said. "I blocked her, and things have been quiet."

Emma was looking at her phone. "Don't be so sure. Check this out."

She held out her phone to show me a post from Sarrah Sleepz. Somehow, she had reposted the selfie of me in my scarf!

That scarf makes me want to barf.

I rolled my eyes. "Wow. Clever."

"There's more," Emma said.

I scrolled through the comments. Olivia had chimed in right away.

Mia is so stuck-up.

"What does that have to do with my scarf?" I wondered out loud.

Then other kids chimed in.

She should pull that scarf over her face.

50

You're not a model, Mia!

Katie and Alexis were looking over Emma's shoulder with me.

"These are even worse than the last ones," Alexis said. "If we want this to stop, we have to find out who Sarrah Sleepz is. It's obviously someone who posted a fake account. My guess is it's one of the BFCs."

Emma frowned. "I could see Olivia doing it, but she's making comments under her own profile. Why would she create a fake profile, too?"

"Good point," Alexis said. "It must be one of the other girls."

"Callie would never do that," said Katie. "And Maggie and Bella are a lot nicer since Sydney moved away."

Sydney Whitman used to be the leader of the BFCs, until she moved to California a while back. We had all been relieved. She had gone out of her way to make our lives miserable.

"It could be anybody," Alexis said. "Anybody can create a fake account. Maybe it's someone from school you don't even know."

"Alexis is right," Katie said. "You need to tell your mom and dad about this."

"Tell them what?" Eddie had walked into the kitchen, just home from work.

"Nothing," I said quickly.

Eddie gave me a look. "Mia, if there's something happening, your parents should know about it."

I knew I wasn't going to be able to wiggle out of this one. "After we're done baking? Please?" I asked, and Eddie nodded, because he is a pretty reasonable guy. He left the kitchen.

"Sorry, Mia," Katie said.

"It's okay," I said. "I don't know what my mom will do, though. Probably flip out."

"Well, I hope somebody can find this Sarrah Sleepz and stop her," Alexis said. "This is one of the worst things about social media. People feel that because they can be anonymous, they can type things onto a screen that they would never say to you in person."

"Definitely," Emma agreed.

I really wanted to stop thinking about Sarrah Sleepz. "Hey, let's make some cupcakes, okay? Eddie needs the kitchen by six to start dinner."

"On it!" Katie said, and she started to pull the mixing bowls out of our cabinet.

Twenty minutes later, Katie's cupcakes were in the oven, and Alexis and Emma had made a frosting flavored with vanilla and more of the cream soda. While the cupcakes baked and cooled, we cleaned up the kitchen.

The cupcakes were ready to frost by five thirty, when Mom got home.

"Something smells good," she said with a smile.

"Cream soda cupcakes," Katie said, holding out a frosted one. "Want to try one?"

Mom held up her hands. "No, thank you. Maybe after dinner if you have some extra."

Alexis cut a finished cupcake into four pieces. "Time for a taste test."

Eddie popped in. "Did somebody say 'taste test'?"

Katie handed him a cupcake. "Let us know if this tastes like cream soda."

Eddie took a bite. He chewed thoughtfully for a minute.

"You're keeping us in suspense!" Katie chided.

Eddie grinned. "I think you've got it. Tastes like cream soda to me."

Katie pumped her fist. "Yes! Gladys will be so happy!"

"Who's Gladys?" Eddie asked.

"She's turning one hundred, and she likes cream soda," I explained.

"Lucky her," Eddie said.

Katie looked at her phone. "My mom will be here in five minutes. Let's tidy up."

We worked quickly to get the dishes put away, and then Mrs. Brown came to drive Katie, Emma, and Alexis home. Then Eddie and Mom came into the kitchen.

"Mia, Eddie says there's something you need to talk to us about," she said. She and Eddie sat down at the kitchen table and motioned for me to do the same.

I felt superuncomfortable. "It's no big deal," I said. "There's this girl on PicPop who's been insulting my selfies."

Mom frowned. "Insulting them how?"

"Just, like, saying stupid things," I replied.

Mom held out her hand. "Can you show me?"

"Well, she's not my PicPop pal anymore because I blocked her," I said. "Maybe I can call it up on Emma's page."

I tapped my screen until I came to the scarf photo, and then I handed the phone to Mom. Her eyes got wide as she read the comments.

"Mia, this is awful!" she said. "I thought PicPop was a safe site."

I shrugged. "I don't know. I guess they just

monitor for bad language and inappropriate photos and stuff."

"But this *is* bad language," Mom said. She handed the photo to Eddie. "Look at this!"

Eddie read the screen, and he looked sad when he was finished. "Oh, Mia, why would anyone say things like this about you? Who is this Sarrah Sleepz?"

"I don't know," I answered. "I friended her a couple of weeks ago because I thought she was from my school, and then she said something mean about this other photo I posted on Monday. So I blocked her."

"Wait one minute," Mom said. "You mean you made friends with someone online who you don't already know?"

"I *thought* I knew her," I said. "I just told you that."

Mom shook her head. "Mia, you know the rules about being online. You can't connect with anybody you don't know. That's a very big safety rule."

"I know, but she was friends with girls from my school," I said. "Like Callie."

"But *you* didn't know her," Mom pointed out. "And I'll bet Callie doesn't know her either. She's obviously using a fake name."

"Lots of people do," I countered.

Mom took the phone from Eddie. "I'm sorry, Mia, but this is serious," she said. She handed the phone back to me. "I want to see you delete your PicPop account. Right now. In front of me."

I couldn't believe it. "What? Are you serious? I did not do anything wrong here! I'm not posting anything I shouldn't!"

"I didn't say you did," Mom said. "The problem is that you weren't careful about who you friended, and now you've become a target of cyberbullying. So please delete it. Now."

Mom's dark eyes were burning through me like lasers. "Fine," I mumbled. "But it's so not fair."

"Then hand me the phone when you're done," she said.

I obeyed. Mom shut off the phone. "Here's what's going to happen: You are going off-line."

"What?" I asked. I was hoping I'd heard her wrong.

"No more Internet," Mom said. "If you go somewhere where I'll need to get in touch with you, you can have your phone back. But only then."

"Mom!" I wailed.

"And I'm confiscating your laptop," she said. "You're not going online on your computer either."

"But that's not fair!" I cried. "I need the Internet for homework! And for Cupcake research and stuff like that!"

"When you've got homework to do, you can use your laptop, but only then," Mom amended.

I looked at Eddie. "This makes no sense! I haven't done anything wrong!"

"Sorry, Mia," Eddie said softly.

My eyes were burning hot with tears. "Fine! Take the stupid laptop!"

I stomped upstairs, got my laptop, then stomped back down and shoved it into her hands.

"Here!" I yelled.

Then I ran upstairs and fell facedown on my bed, crying.

I had figured that Mom would flip out when she found out about Sarrah Sleepz. I thought maybe she'd call the school or something, to try to find out who Sarrah was. I didn't in a million years think she would end up punishing me.

It was so unfair!

CHAPTER 7

Things Get Even Worse!

It's so unfair," I told Katie on the bus the next morning (in a loud whisper, because I didn't want anyone else to hear me). "Why would she take away my phone? I'm not the one harassing people!"

Katie shook her head sympathetically. "That makes no sense," she replied. "Unless she's trying to protect you or something."

"I don't need protecting," I told her. "It's just some mean comments. I can deal with that."

"I know, but they were starting to get, like, *really* mean," Katie said.

I didn't say anything. I wasn't going to let it get to me, no matter what.

Then Katie's eyes got wide. "Hey, does this mean you can't sleep over tonight?"

I frowned. "I don't know. Mom didn't say I was grounded, just that I couldn't use my phone or laptop. I would text to her to ask, but I don't have my phone!"

Katie took out hers. "I'll text my mom and ask her to text your mom." She started typing quickly.

I shook my head. "Do you see how ridiculous this is? If I had my phone, I could just ask her."

Katie looked up from her phone. "Mom says she'll ask."

"Great," I said flatly. "How am I supposed to get through the day without my phone?"

Katie turned hers off. "Well, we can't use them during class, anyway," she pointed out. "Don't worry. The day will go really fast."

Luckily, Katie was right. During class I didn't think about my phone, and at lunchtime, Katie turned on her phone and smiled as she read her messages.

"Your mom says you can still sleep over," she reported.

That made me feel better. At least I had something fun to look forward to.

After school I packed my overnight bag as quickly as I could. Dan knocked on my door.

"Sara says I'm supposed to drive you to Katie's

right now," he said. "Are you ready to go?"

Sara is my mom's name, so that's what Dan calls her, just like I call his father Eddie. But it still sounds weird to me to hear Dan call my mom by her first name. For the first time, I wondered if hearing me call his dad Eddie made him feel weird too.

"Thanks!" I called out. "I'm almost done packing."

I was relieved that Dan was the one driving me, and not Mom or Eddie. I was still pretty mad at both of them.

"I heard about your phone," Dan said, and I felt uncomfortable. Was he going to rub it in my face?

"That's pretty unfair," he continued, surprising me. "I'm sorry."

"Thanks," I said, nodding gratefully.

And that's all we said about it, but that was enough for me. His car was an old one of Eddie's, and it had a CD player in it. Dan slipped in a disc. I braced myself for heavy metal music, but instead, La Vida Pasa blared out of the speakers. It was the first song on their latest album, *Cuando ella me mira*, which means "when she looks at me."

I smiled at Dan. "Thanks," I said. I know he was mostly playing it because I was in the car.

"It's a good song," he said.

The music was blaring when we pulled up in front of Katie's house. She ran out to meet me.

"Is this that band you like?" she yelled over the music.

I nodded and then turned to Dan. "Thanks!"

Dan waved and drove off, and Katie hugged me. "Yay! Sleepover!" she cheered. "Come on inside."

I followed her in, and she was talking a mile a minute. "Mom's not home yet, but she said we could order anything we wanted for dinner. So I have menus for Thai, Chinese, Italian, subs, and Indian. I'm not sure what I'm in the mood for."

"Well, I—" I began, but Katie kept talking.

"Mom also said we could rent a movie after dinner, but I'm not sure what we should watch. I kind of want to see *Sky Zone* again, but that new movie about the food truck owners who fall in love is out."

"I actually like—" I began again.

"And I almost forgot! We got stuff for ice-cream sundaes!" Katie interrupted me as we walked up to her room. "Including the hot fudge you put in the microwave. Although I was thinking maybe caramel. Or I guess we could combine both. That would be good."

She stopped and looked at me. "What's so

funny? You've got a big grin on your face."

"You!" I said. I picked up a purple pillow from her floor and bopped her with it. "Excited, much?"

Katie grabbed the pillow from me and bopped me back. "Sorry! We almost never get to do a sleepover. I'm so excited that I could sing."

She picked up a hairbrush from her dresser and started to sing the tune to "Cuando ella me mira." Except she didn't really know the words.

"Wando aya mermaid!" she sang.

I shook my head, laughing. "It's *'cuanda ella me mira,'*" I corrected her.

Katie picked up her phone. "How do you spell the band's name again?"

I told her, and she brought up the video for the song and started to blast it. Soon, we were jumping up and down and dancing like crazy. When the song ended, Katie collapsed on the bed.

"That was awesome!" she said. "I get it now. You don't have to know the words to like the song. But I understood some of it. It's about some girl. And he feels crazy."

I nodded. "The song's not too complicated. He feels crazy when the girl looks at him, and he sings about it. Most of the songs are like that."

Katie picked up her phone again and showed

me a picture of the band. "Okay, so tell me who they are."

"Okay, so the one with the long hair is Mateo. He sings lead," I said. "Then there's David and Ian and Gabriel. David sometimes plays guitar, but mostly, they all sing. I think Mateo's the cutest."

Katie pointed to Ian. "I think I like him best. He has big eyes."

She started scrolling through the screen. "Let me find another song."

Pop! Pop!

"Is that PicPop?" I asked, curious.

Katie nodded. "I posted a photo of all the take-out menus earlier."

She opened the app. "Everyone's voting for us to get Indian food," she said, and then her face clouded.

"What is it?" I asked.

Katie sighed. "I friended Sarrah Sleepz because I wanted to make sure she wasn't still being mean to you. But she is."

"Let me see!" I said quickly—which made me wonder why I was so curious to see what Sarrah Sleepz had done next. But I was! I couldn't help it.

Sarrah had posted a photo of me at school that day.

"Oh no!" I cried. "Is she secretly taking photos of me now?"

I was feeling angry that morning so I wore a red sweater with a short black skirt and red tights, and my new boots. I thought I looked angry and cute at the same time.

She looks like a checkerboard! Sarrah Sleepz had written.

Olivia had been the first to chime in. **Red is a bad color for her. But so is every color!**

The next comment was from Maggie. It was an emoji of a smiley face with swirly eyes. **Hurts to look at!** she wrote.

"Maggie?" I said. She was one of the nicer girls in the BFC. I expected it from Olivia, and I didn't care about the people I didn't even know. But I thought I was cool with Maggie.

Katie put her hand on my shoulder. "This stinks, Mia! I'm going to write something." She reached for the phone.

"No!" I cried, holding the phone out of her

reach. "I mean, that's nice of you to want to help. But you can't get into it with them. It won't solve anything. And then they'll start attacking you too."

Katie frowned. "I guess you're right. Besides, I don't even think I could think up mean things to say."

I handed her the phone. "Forget them. They're just being dumb. So what did you say about Indian food?"

Katie jumped up. "I'll get the menu!" she cried. "You know, one of the food trucks in that movie is an Indian food truck, so we could have a theme night. This is perfect! I'll be right back."

Katie raced off, excited about the sleepover again. And the rest of the night was awesome. I discovered that I love tandoori chicken. I remembered how sweet romantic comedies are. I tasted the great combination of hot fudge and caramel.

When Katie and I finally drifted off to sleep that night, I realized I hadn't thought about Sarrah Sleepz once the whole time. I was almost grateful that Mom had taken away my phone—almost.

CHAPTER 8

I Can't Take It Anymore!

$\mathcal{D}$o you really think I would lie about having homework just to get my laptop back?"

It was Saturday afternoon, and the glow of the awesome sleepover with Katie had faded. I was back home, arguing with Mom again about electronics.

"I just want to see your assignments, Mia," Mom said. "I have a right to ask."

"Well, good luck with that. I need to get on the school website to show you," I snapped. Yes, I know I wasn't being nice, but honestly, Mom was going too far with the whole security thing!

Mom didn't respond to my snippiness. She walked out of the kitchen and came back a minute later with my laptop. She set it down in front of me.

"Okay. Show me."

I logged in and went to the Park Street Middle School website.

"See?" I showed Mom. "I've got to go to the math website and do two work sheets, print out the vocabulary work sheet, and I have to find five sources for my report on the Civil War."

Mom looked over my shoulder. "Okay. But I don't want you visiting other sites, okay?"

"What about fashion sites? And cupcake sites?" I asked. "Everything I need to do is on the Internet, Mom. That's just how it is these days."

Mom sighed. "I'll tell you what: You get four hours of laptop time today and four hours tomorrow. Use them wisely. Don't give me a reason not to trust you."

"I never did," I mumbled, and luckily, Mom didn't jump on me for that. I closed up my laptop and went upstairs to my room.

I got to work on my math, and after about an hour, I stopped for a break to stretch and get some water. When I got back to the computer, I noticed the PicPop icon still up on my screen from when I'd last opened it. It was tempting to click on it.

I paused. Mom was downstairs in her office. My bedroom door was closed. How would she know?

I quickly opened the PicPop site on my computer. I didn't have a profile anymore, so I just scrolled through the feed, looking at my friends' photos.

I saw a photo of Callie with Olivia, Maggie, and Bella. I couldn't help myself. I had to know if they were still talking trash about me with Sarrah Sleepz. I typed in Callie's name so I could look at her pics.

Sarrah hadn't put up any new photos of me, but there were lots of comments on the ones of me in my red shirt and tights.

Not-so-super girl!

A tomato with legs!

Then Sarrah had added: Can't wait 2 c what Misfit Mia will do next!

I quickly clicked out of the app like I was backing away from a poisonous snake. My face was hot with anger. This whole thing was really starting to get to me! But I could never tell Mom now, or she'd know that I'd peeked.

Think, Mia, I told myself. *There's got to be a way*

to stop this. Sarrah will keep making fun of everything you wear. Unless . . .

That's when it hit me. If I didn't wear anything outrageous, I reasoned, Sarrah would have nothing to comment about. I opened my closet. What was the most basic thing I had? What did the girls at my school wear every day? Skinny jeans, of course. And those boots with the fur sticking out were still all the rage at my school, for some reason. I could pair them with a plain black T-shirt and wear my hair down. No braids.

So that's what I did. On Monday morning, I wore that exact outfit, an outfit that was guaranteed to make me blend in with just about every other girl at Park Street Middle School—except for Katie, who liked bright colors, and Alexis, who always looked ready for a business meeting, and Emma, who preferred dresses most of the time. Hmm. Maybe that's why we were all friends!

As I got ready for school, I tried Mom one more time. "So, can I please have my phone back today?"

"No," Mom said. "And stop asking. You'll get it back when I feel you're ready to get it back."

I glared at her and ate my breakfast in silence. Knowing Mom, I wouldn't get my phone back until I was as old as Gladys Bailey!

So, even though I hate Mondays (I know I've said that before, but I'll never stop saying it), the morning went pretty smoothly. I felt like a ninja, walking through the halls in my T-shirt and skinny jeans. Looking around, half the girls had on the same outfit. I felt relieved. No one could make fun of me today.

I have outsmarted Sarrah Sleepz, I thought, but boy, was I wrong.

At lunchtime I was talking with Katie, Emma, and Alexis when I noticed something. Some kids at the next table were pointing at our table and laughing.

"What's their problem?" I asked, pointing a chin toward their table. I looked around the cafeteria. Over at the BFC table, Olivia was looking right at me while she whispered to Maggie.

My stomach dropped. "Oh no. Again?"

"You mean you think Sarrah Sleepz posted another photo?" Katie asked, and I nodded.

"Let me check," Emma said, taking out her phone.

She quickly scrolled through her screen and then frowned.

"Let me see," I insisted, holding out my hand.

Emma handed me her phone, and Katie looked

over my shoulder. Sarrah Sleepz had snapped another photo of me from just this morning!

Look who just woke up! This outfit makes me want to go back to sleep.

Someone else wrote under her: Those boots are so last year! Nice try, but you're out of step, Mia!

I looked around the cafeteria. So many girls were wearing those boots! That's why I had put them on. Why was Sarrah singling me out?

Alexis had called up the picture on her phone. "Enough of this," she said, standing up.

"What are you doing?" I asked.

Alexis walked toward the BFC table. I moved to go with her, but Emma put her hand on my arm.

"Let her do this," Emma said.

Alexis stood in front of the BFC table, her arms folded. "All right. Which one of you is Sarrah Sleepz?"

Olivia's eyes got wide. "Who's that?"

"You know who that is," Alexis said, "so don't bother to lie about it. It's obviously a fake account, and one of you must have started it." She looked right at Olivia when she said it.

I noticed that Callie was looking down at her sandwich, and Maggie and Bella were giggling. Olivia raised her right hand.

"I solemnly swear that nobody at this table created the Sarrah Sleepz account," she said.

Alexis glared at her. "Well, if you didn't, then you know who did. So you'd better tell her to cut it out."

"Why should we do that?" Olivia shot back.

"Because it's not nice," Alexis said. She looked at Callie now. "You know it's not."

Then Alexis turned and marched back to our table. Katie starting clapping.

"Go, Alexis!" she cheered.

"You didn't have to do that," I said.

"Yes, I did," Alexis said. "You're my friend, Mia, and what's happening is wrong."

She picked up her phone. "I'm going to report those comments to the PicPop staff. There's got to be a way to shut down Sarrah Sleepz."

"I'll report her too," Katie said, and Emma picked up her phone and started typing as well.

Right then I felt so grateful to have such good friends! For a second I wondered why it even mattered what Sarrah and those other girls said about me when I had Katie, Emma, and Alexis around me.

But I had to be honest with myself. It did hurt. Every new comment was starting to feel like a slap.

"This is going too far," Katie said as she typed. "It has to be having an effect on you."

I nodded. "It has. I even wore what I thought was a boring outfit today so that Sarrah would leave me alone."

"Don't you get it? It doesn't matter what you wear. She's going to come after you no matter what," Alexis said fiercely.

"I know," I said, and I felt tears in the back of my eyes again. "I just don't know what to do. When I told my mom, she just took away my phone. That didn't help."

"That was before it got really bad," Katie pointed out. "You should talk to her again."

"Maybe," I said, but I was convinced it was no use. Mom would probably just lock me in my room and throw away the key!

CHAPTER 9

This Is Messing with My Head!

No school tomorrow!" Katie announced when she boarded the bus the next morning.

"Good," I said, relieved. That was one less day that Sarrah Sleepz could post a photo of me.

George leaned over the seat behind us. "A bunch of us are going to see that movie *Pool Party* tonight. You guys should come."

Katie made a face. "Is that the one about those high school kids who work at a swim club? It looks kind of dumb."

"What else are you going to see? *Ninja Giraffe 2?*" George asked.

"Why not?" Katie countered. "*Ninja Giraffe* was really funny. Remember when he fought all those monkeys?"

George struck a martial arts pose with his arms. "No more monkeying around!" Katie cracked up.

"Seriously, though," George said. "You guys should go see *Pool Party*. Everyone's going to be there."

I looked at Katie. "Come on! It will be fun."

Katie sighed. "Fine. I can see *Ninja Giraffe 2* some other time."

But our moms had a different idea.

"Absolutely not!" Mom said when I brought up the subject after school that day. "That movie is PG-13."

"So?" I shot back. "So are all those vampire movies. You let me go see those."

"This is different," Mom said. "Sharon and I talked about it. Movies get PG-13 ratings for different reasons. And I don't think a movie about a wild high school party is appropriate for you and Katie."

"But everyone in school is seeing it!" I said, and I could hear my voice getting loud. "Everyone!"

"That is between them and their parents," Mom said. "Case closed. But if you and Katie want to go see *Ninja Giraffe 2*, I will drive you there."

I didn't want to go see some dumb cartoon movie—no offense to Katie, but I didn't. However, the thought of staying in the house with my mom was worse. I was going to the movies.

"Fine," I mumbled.

Mom and I didn't talk much after that, but she did take Katie and me to the Royal Theater, which is attached to the mall, later that night.

Inside, it was pretty crowded with people taking advantage of a no-school-tomorrow-Tuesday by going to the movies. We waited in line for the box office and then got our tickets for *Ninja Giraffe 2*.

"Can you believe our moms?" I said. "Like, suddenly we're not old enough to see a PG–13 movie? How random is that?"

"Well, Mom has never let me see just any PG–13 movie," Katie explained. "She reads the reviews first. It was probably her idea."

"Well, my mom went along with it," I said.

"Hey, cheer up!" Katie said, lightly punching me in the arm. "I promise you that *Ninja Giraffe 2* will be fun." We handed our tickets to the ticket taker and got our stubs.

"Now let's get candy and mix it in with our popcorn," Katie said. Katie has discovered this thing where she takes those small chocolate candies studded with white dots and mixes them into her popcorn. When you take a bite of popcorn, you get some chocolate with it. It's actually pretty good.

"Hey, Katie! Mia!"

It was George.

"Hey, George!" Katie called back.

"Shhh!" I said, nudging her. "Don't tell him we're going to see *Ninja Giraffe 2.*"

"Why not?" Katie asked.

I looked around. There were lots of kids from our school there. George was with his friends Wes and Jacob. By a corner I could see Maggie and Bella with some other girls from school. And there were more kids around too.

What if one of them was Sarrah Sleepz? What if somebody took a picture of me going into the *Ninja Giraffe 2* theater? I could just imagine what Sarrah would have to say about that.

"Just don't," I hissed to Katie. George ran up to us with a big grin on his face.

"You guys gonna sit with us?" he asked.

"Actually—" Katie began, but I interrupted her.

"Sure," I said.

Katie looked at me, her eyes wide. "Mia . . ."

I grabbed her by the arm. "We'll be right back," I told George, and then I dragged her away.

"Let's just go see *Pool Party*," I said. "Everyone

else is doing it. It will look weird if we go see the other movie."

Katie frowned. "But we bought our tickets for *Ninja Giraffe 2*. Isn't that illegal or something?"

"No way," I said. "People do it all the time. Come on. It'll be fine. Besides, won't it be more fun to watch a movie with George?"

Katie looked over at the ticket taker. "Are you sure we won't get in trouble?" she asked, and I knew I had convinced her.

"Of course not," I said, and I took her by the arm again. "Let's go!"

We followed George and his friends inside the theater. They all wanted to sit in the very back row. Katie sat between me and George.

The previews started playing, and George, Wes, and Jacob were totally loud and rowdy during them. In this one preview a guy jumped out of a plane and landed on a moving train below.

"Yeah! Awesome!" cheered Wes.

"That would be, like, totally impossible," I whispered to Katie.

Then they showed a preview for a romantic movie, and when the couple kissed, the boys started yelling again. It was really annoying.

"Woooooooooooo!" George hooted, and even

though it was dark, I was sure Katie was blushing.

Finally, the movie started, and the boys quieted down, thankfully. It was about these kids who work at a swim club, and at night, when the club closes, they have this huge party. There were a lot of dumb jokes and girls in bikinis and teenagers making out.

Why did I want to see this movie? I asked myself, but I knew the answer. I didn't want anyone to think I was an immature kid by going to see a cartoon movie about a giraffe. So the real question was, when did I start caring about what other people thought?

When the movie ended, the lights came on.

"That was funny," George said.

Katie shrugged. "I guess." She turned to me. "Come on, Mia."

This time, Katie pulled *me* by the arm. She dragged me out of the theater.

"That was awful!" she said when we got to the lobby. "Everyone in that movie was acting so dumb."

"Yeah, you're right," I admitted.

"You know, now I have to wait until *Ninja Giraffes 2* comes out on DVD before I can see it," Katie said, annoyed. "And I'll have to lie to my mom when she asks me how it was. Why exactly did we go see that dumb movie again?"

"I'm sorry," I said. "It's Sarrah Sleepz. She's messing with my head. I thought somebody might take a picture of me going into the movie, and it's, like, a kid's movie, and I thought she would make fun of me."

Katie shook her head. "Wow, Mia, this is really affecting you. You've got to do something about it!"

I nodded. Katie was right. I didn't like how Sarrah was making me feel. I was becoming not-Mia. I needed to be Mia again.

"I know, but what am I supposed to do?" I asked. Then I remembered something. "What happened when you reported her to PicPop?"

Kate's face clouded. "They messaged me back and said that because the comments didn't use 'inappropriate language,' they couldn't remove them or stop her. And I messaged them back, like, you mean being mean to someone isn't inappropriate? But they didn't respond."

My heart sank. There was no way to stop Sarrah Sleepz. She was going to be making my life miserable forever!

CHAPTER 10

There's Hope!

"How was the movie?" Mom asked when she picked up me and Katie.

I looked at Katie. She was biting her lip, and I could tell she didn't want to lie.

"Really cute," I answered for us. "You know I love giraffes."

That seemed to satisfy Mom, who chatted with Katie on the way to Katie's house. After we dropped off Katie, Mom and I were quiet on the way home. Things were pretty tense between us.

And it's all Sarrah Sleepz's fault, I couldn't help thinking. *None of this would be happening if she hadn't started picking on me!*

Then another little voice in my head chimed in. *And if you hadn't friended her on PicPop. Maybe Mom was right about friending people you don't know. . . .*

I knew that little voice was probably right, but it didn't make me feel any better. When we got home, I mumbled good night and headed upstairs to my room.

The nice thing about having a day off from school is that I didn't have to set the alarm. I slept . . . and slept . . . and slept. When I finally woke up, it was almost eleven o'clock!

I reached to check my phone, out of habit, and remembered it wasn't there. With a sigh, I got out of bed and made my way to the bathroom.

When I finally got downstairs, Mom was in the kitchen, making sandwiches.

"Good *almost afternoon*," she said, emphasizing the last two words to make a point that I'd slept so late.

"Hi," I said groggily. I reached into the fridge and pulled out the water pitcher.

"I made egg salad," Mom said.

"You're working here today?" I asked. Since Mom is a fashion stylist, she doesn't work for anyone specific—she has different clients. Sometimes she's out all day meeting with them, and other days she stays home, working in her home office.

Mom nodded. "Yes. Eddie's at work, and Dan

went to play basketball down at the park, so it's just you and me."

I sat down, and Mom slid a plate over to me. There was definitely an awkward tension between us. I was relieved when the doorbell rang.

"Who could that be?" Mom asked, and I jumped up to answer it.

To my surprise, it was Katie and her mom.

"Oh, hi!" I said.

"Hi, Mia," Mrs. Brown said. "I know this is unexpected, but may we come in?"

"Sure," I said, looking at Katie, hoping to get some clue as to why they were there. But Katie just kind of nervously looked away.

Mom got up from her chair, and she hugged Mrs. Brown.

"What a nice surprise, Sharon!" Mom said.

"I hope this isn't a bad time," said Mrs. Brown. "But Katie told me something, and I thought it was important to talk to you in person about it."

For a second I couldn't breathe. Katie had told her mom about Sarrah Sleepz! I wasn't sure if I felt angry or relieved. Katie was pacing back and forth in the kitchen.

"Is that egg salad?" Katie asked, eyeing the bowl on the counter.

"Katie, manners!" her mom scolded.

"No, that's fine. Katie, help yourself," Mom said. "Now, Sharon, please sit down and tell me what's happening."

Mrs. Brown sat next to my mom. She's got brown hair, like Katie, but she wears it cut short—stylishly short, because my mom picked out the haircut for her.

"I think you know part of the story," Mrs. Brown said. "A girl on the PicPop app has been making fun of Mia."

Mom nodded. "Yes, I know. I had Mia delete the app from her phone."

"I understand," said Mrs. Brown. "But Katie tells me that the problem hasn't stopped. This girl, who calls herself Sarrah Sleepz, has been posting photos of Mia and making mean comments. And other girls from the school are chiming in."

"Oh no!" Mom said. She looked at me. "Mia, why didn't you tell me?"

"I *did* tell you," I said. "And you took away my phone. So I figured there was no point in telling you again."

Mom suddenly looked very sad. "I thought that would be the end of it, Mia. I'm sorry. Katie, can you show me what's been happening?"

Katie put down the egg salad sandwich she had just made, found Sarrah Sleepz's PicPop profile, and handed her phone to my mom. Mom scrolled through the page, shaking her head.

"This is awful!" she said. "How is she getting photos of you when you're not her friend?"

"She's probably someone from our school with a fake account, but we don't know who it is," Katie said. "And Alexis, Emma, and I reported it to PicPop, but they said it's not inappropriate and they can't take it down."

Mom looked at Mrs. Brown. "Surely the school can do something."

"That's what I was thinking," Katie's mom replied. "Park Street Middle School has an anti-bullying policy, including cyberbullying, and if this person is a student at the school, it would apply to him or her."

That idea made me nervous. "What if she gets in big trouble? Won't she just target me more?"

"We'll do everything we can to make sure that doesn't happen," Mom promised. "But it's clear that we need to do something. This can't go on anymore."

A wave of relief washed over me then, hearing Mom say that. She was on my side. So was Mrs. Brown. And my friends. For the first time I had hope that the Sarrah Sleepz thing would end.

Mom hugged me. "The school is closed today, but I'll call first thing in the morning."

"Thanks, Mom," I said, my voice muffled because she was squeezing me to tightly.

She released me and looked me in the eyes. "And I hope you know, Mia, that none of those things those girls are writing are true. You are beautiful and wonderful, and I would hate to see you lose confidence because of some online comments."

Tears sprang into my eyes. "Thanks."

"We should leave you two alone," Mrs. Brown said, standing up.

"Buddd mmmm stillll eating," Katie protested, her mouth full of egg salad.

"How can you eat an egg salad sandwich during a touching moment like this?" I teased her.

Katie shrugged and swallowed. "I can't help it. Your mom's egg salad is awesome!"

She and her mom said their good-byes and left.

"So does this mean I can get my phone and laptop back?" I asked Mom.

"I still need to think about that," Mom said. "I am not saying that what has happened is your fault. But the Internet is not a safe place. I didn't do a good job of protecting you."

I just nodded. I didn't want to argue, and I had a feeling she was coming around, so I didn't want to spoil it.

Then Mom's face brightened. "Want to go to the mall? I feel like shopping."

"Definitely!" I said. "Just let me finish my awesome egg salad."

So Mom and I had a fun afternoon at the mall. First, we stopped at the craft store, so I could get what I needed for the birthday cupcakes the Cupcake Club was working on. I had come up some with new ideas, and I just needed the materials to make them real.

Mom also bought me some new clothes: a cute button-up cardigan that would be great for layering; a long-sleeved knit top with a scoop neck; and a sweet-looking scarf. Plus three more pairs of tights.

The next morning I put all my new stuff together with a pair of skinny jeans, and I loved how it looked—except for my hair. I was wearing it down, and I wanted something more fun to go with the look. So I put my hair in the low-hanging braids again.

"Bring it on, Sarrah Sleepz!" I said as I looked in the mirror. I was back to the old Mia—not caring what anyone thought. I felt really good.

As I strolled through the halls of the school that morning, I tried to keep an eye out to see if anyone was taking my picture. But the halls of Park Street Middle School get so crowded between classes that it was really hard to tell if someone was trying to sneak a pic of me. I would have to wait until lunch.

"Yup," said Katie, looking at her phone after we sat down in the cafeteria. "She's got a picture of you in your outfit this morning."

Nice scarf, loser! Sarrah had commented.

"Wow, she's not even trying to be clever anymore," I said.

"Who's not trying to be clever?" Alexis asked as she and Emma walked up with their lunch trays.

"Sarrah Sleepz," I said. "She's at it again."

"But not for long," Katie said, and she lowered her voice. "Mia's mom is going to call the school this morning. So it's only a matter of time before we find out who she is."

"Do you think they can find out? I hope so," Emma said.

Alexis looked around. "I hope so too. Everybody is way too interested in this."

I followed her gaze. All around us, kids were

looking at their phones and then looking at me. A lot of them were laughing. Enough was enough!

I'd had it. I raised my voice loud enough for other kids to hear. "You know, I wonder why Sarrah Sleepz keeps wasting her time. She must have nothing better to do. And neither does anybody who follows her."

My heart was pounding. The cafeteria got a little quiet. Then I heard applause. George and his friends were clapping.

"You tell 'em, Mia!" George called out.

Then Sophie and Lucy walked up to our table.

"Mia, it is totally wrong what is happening to you," Sophie said.

"Yeah, totally wrong," echoed Lucy. "And most people are on your side."

"They think it's mean," said Sophie.

I nodded. "Thanks."

Sophie and Lucy walked away, and I let out a deep breath. "That felt good," I said.

"You are so brave!" said Katie.

"I can't wait until they unmask Sarrah Sleepz," Alexis said. "I hope she gets suspended and this goes on her permanent record!"

"I just hope she stops being mean to Mia," Emma said.

I smiled at my friends. "Have I told you guys lately that you're the best? Because you are!"

"We're your friends. We're supposed to be the best," Alexis said. She took out her phone. "So, I don't mean to change the subject, but we've got a busy Saturday coming up. Evan Smith's party is at three, and Gladys Bailey's party is at five. I still think we should bake Friday night and decorate Saturday morning."

"I can't help you bake tomorrow night," I said. "I have the concert. Normally, I'd be with dad anyway this weekend, but he's letting me stay with Mom since there's so much going on. So I can definitely decorate on Saturday."

Katie looked at Alexis. "We can't bake on Friday," she said.

Alexis frowned. "Why not?"

Emma nudged her. "We can't. Remember?"

Alexis's eyes got wide, and she nodded. "Oh right. Of course. Sure, we'll bake Saturday morning. Katie, how early can we come to your house?"

"As early as we need to," Katie said.

At the time I thought all this was a little weird. Were my friends keeping a secret from me? But it didn't seem like a big deal, so I didn't dwell on it.

"My mom and I picked up what we need for

the decorations at the mall yesterday," I said, and I took out my sketchbook and started touching up my finished cupcake designs. They were really cute. I couldn't wait to see how they'd look on Saturday.

It was nice to have something else to think about besides Sarrah Sleepz! All in all, it had been a pretty good day. It was the nicest one I had in a while at least.

CHAPTER 11

Things Heat Up, but I Keep My Cool!

When I got back from school that day, there was a note from Mom on the kitchen table.

Mia,

I called the school this morning, and they took the situation very seriously. They are looking into it. I have a client meeting tonight, and Eddie is working late. Dan and Sebastian will be around. There is chicken and rice in the fridge that you can microwave and stuff for a salad.

Love you so much!

Mom

PS Don't forget to feed Tiki and Milkshake.

My two little dogs were yapping at my feet, trying to climb up on me.

"How could I forget to feed you two?" I said in that high voice I use when I talk to my dogs. I scooped them up. "You'd never let me forget!"

I sat down on the couch with the dogs and pet them both for a little while, enjoying the peace and quiet of the house. Then Dan and Sebastian burst in, shattering the silence.

"That new bass riff is sweet!" Sebastian was saying, high-fiving Dan.

"I know. We are going to kill it!" Dan countered.

"Mom and Eddie aren't here," I told them. "Mom left us some food to microwave for dinner. She said there's stuff for salad, so I guess *I'll* be the one making it, unless one of you wants to?"

"Whatever," Dan said, and then he and Sebastian disappeared into the basement to practice their music. I braced myself for the worst.

I knew what was coming, and that it was going to be loud, so I went upstairs to do my homework. I put on my headphones and plugged them into my mp3 player. Thankfully, Mom hadn't taken that away too.

Around six o'clock I started feeling hungry, so I went downstairs. The sound of heavy metal music was blaring from the basement.

"I'll make dinner myself," I told Tiki and Milkshake as I filled their bowls with food.

Then I made a salad out of bagged lettuce, tomatoes, and cucumbers. I pulled out the plastic container of the chicken and rice and stuck it into the microwave. Mom had a note on it that it would take about ten minutes.

When the microwave bell dinged, I braced myself and went downstairs. Dan was playing bass, and Sebastian was drumming along to a very loud song blaring from Dan's music player.

"Dinner's ready!" I yelled.

Sebastian turned his head to look at me.

"I said, dinner's ready!" I yelled again.

"Sorry, *chica*!" Sebastian yelled back. "We can't stop now. We are on fire!"

I shook my head. "Whatever."

I climbed back upstairs and fixed myself a plate

of chicken and rice and salad. It was weird eating alone, so I went into the living room. I hardly ever watch TV anymore, but without my phone and laptop, what else was I supposed to do? I clicked it on and lucked out with a marathon of *Real Teens of Southern Cali.*

I hadn't seen the show in ages, and I'd forgotten how addictive it was. It was all about these rich kids in California who were always fighting with one another and wearing fabulous clothes. The music coming from the basement was so loud that I couldn't hear what anyone was saying, so I turned on the closed-captioning and settled in.

I was almost three episodes in when the music stopped and Dan and Sebastian emerged from the basement.

"We're starving!" Dan said.

I nodded toward the kitchen. "You'll have to heat up the chicken and rice again. And there's salad."

They disappeared into the kitchen, and a few minutes later, I heard pots and pans banging around. Curious, I paused the TV, and then I got up to see what they were up to.

Dan was holding a carton of eggs, and Sebastian was putting strips of bacon into a pan on the stovetop. I could see that the flame on the pan was up really high.

"What are you doing?" I asked.

"We don't have chicken-and-rice hunger—we have bacon hunger," Dan replied.

"Bacon!" Sebastian cheered. He dropped in another bacon slice, and grease splattered out.

Then the pan caught on fire! Orange flames leaped up, and Sebastian jumped back.

Dan yelled out a curse word and raced to the sink. He grabbed a pot from the drain board and started to fill it with water. But I'd had enough kitchen time with Katie and the Cupcake Club to know what to do.

"No!" I yelled. I took a cover from the cupboard and covered the flaming pan with it. "It's a grease fire. Only oxygen will put it out. Water will make it worse."

Smoke billowed up from under the bacon pan, filling the kitchen. Tiki and Milkshake started yapping like crazy. Dan ran to open a window.

Sebastian looked shaken. He hugged me. "You saved us, Mia!"

"What is going on here?"

Eddie and Mom walked into the kitchen. Eddie quickly figured out what was happening and ran to the stove. He lifted up the pot to reveal the burned bacon underneath.

"I made you chicken and rice! Why were you cooking bacon?" Mom asked. "Mia, didn't you get my note?"

I was about to respond when Dan chimed in.

"It wasn't Mia's fault," he said. "She told us to eat the chicken and rice. But we wanted bacon. I'm sorry."

"And Mia saved the day," Sebastian added. "Dan almost put water on it, but Mia put the pot on it instead."

"Right. You never put water on a grease fire," Eddie said. He looked at the boys. "I'm disappointed in you two. But I'm glad everyone's all right."

"Good work, Mia," Mom said. "You kept calm and did the right thing."

"Yeah," I said. "It's a good thing I'm going to the concert with these two. They'll need someone to protect them."

Mom smiled at me, and we all got to work cleaning up the kitchen.

"You two, microwave yourselves some chicken and rice," Mom told Dan and Sebastian. "Mia, may Eddie and I please speak with you in the dining room? It's important."

Uh-oh, I thought. Usually, when two parents want to speak with you, it's never good. But both of them were smiling.

"Eddie and I have been discussing your phone and laptop," Mom said. "And now I'm more sure than ever that we've made the right decision. I'm very proud of the way you handled yourself tonight, but also for the way you handled yourself with the cyberbully. You didn't respond back, or try to get revenge, or return mean comments. That was very mature of you."

Mature! She had called me mature! I couldn't believe it.

"So we've decided to trust you a little more," Mom said. "But I hope you'll use better judgment when connecting with people on the Internet next time. And we'll be monitoring your accounts to make sure you're not getting into any bad situations again."

I nodded. "Yeah, I understand." And I did. Friending someone I didn't know had brought me nothing but trouble.

"So you can have your phone and laptop back," Mom said.

"Now?" I asked.

"Sure, now," she replied.

"Do you mind if I get them from you a little later?" I asked. "I'm watching *Real Teens of Southern Cali,* and I need to know if Risa and Jared are going to get back together."

Mom and Eddie looked at each other.

"Wow, I thought you'd be scrambling to get them back," Eddie said.

I shrugged. "I guess I learned I can live without them," I said, and then I quickly realized that it was dangerous for them to know that. "But not for too long."

"Of course not," Mom said. She stood up and then came over and kissed me on the forehead. "Oh dear. You smell like bacon."

"We all smell like bacon," I told her.

"It could be worse," Eddie said. "I read that there's a cologne out there that smells like bacon. People like the smell."

"Not *burned* bacon," Mom said.

I left them to argue about bacon and returned to the living room to watch one more episode of *Real Teens.* Then I got my phone back from Mom and took a picture of the pan of burned bacon. I texted it to Katie.

Saved the house from burning down. Got my phone back. Feel like a superhero!

Mighty Mia! Katie texted back. Is everyone okay?

Everyone's fine, I replied.

Mighty Mia. I liked the sound of that. Mighty Mia, facing the evil supervillain Sarrah Sleepz.

Things were almost back to normal, but my adventures were not over. I still had cupcakes to bake—and a supervillain to unmask.

CHAPTER 12

And the Real Sarrah Sleepz Is . . .

So you put the fire out by yourself?" Katie asked me as we rode the bus the next day.

"It wasn't so hard," I admitted. "I remembered what you had told me about grease fires that time we were making maple bacon cupcakes. Dan was going to throw water on the fire, but I covered it with a pot lid instead."

Katie leaned over the backseat to look at George. "Did you hear that? Mia is a hero!"

"Now you're exaggerating," I told Katie.

"Well, you're my hero, anyway," Katie said.

George groaned. "You two are too cute for this early in the morning!"

The bus pulled up to the school, and I headed for homeroom. I was wearing my braids again, and part of me was still nervous about what Sarrah Sleepz might be posting about me.

A quiz in first-period math helped me take my mind off things. Then in Ms. Harmeyer's English class we had reading time, and that helped too.

Things started to get interesting in third-period gym. We had all changed into our shorts and T-shirts. Ms. Chen had us doing laps around the gym when Mrs. DeCaro, one of the women who works in the front office, came in. She whispered to Ms. Chen.

"Callie! Bella!" Ms. Chen called out.

The two girls broke away from the line of runners and jogged over to Ms. Chen. She said something to them, and then they left with Mrs. DeCaro.

Alexis caught up to me. "I bet this has something to do with Sarrah Sleepz," she whispered. "Callie and Bella both commented on those photos of you. They're definitely suspects."

"You sound like a detective," I told her.

Alexis frowned. "I wish I were. Then maybe I could solve this for you. But I have a feeling you'll have your answer soon."

She was right. After gym we had lunch, and I had just taken a bite out of my salad when Callie walked up to our table.

"I need to talk to you," she said, and she had a serious look on her face.

"Uh, sure," I said. I stood up because I got the feeling she wanted to talk to me privately. We walked to an empty table in a corner of the lunchroom. Callie started to nervously twist a strand of her blond hair around her finger.

"So, listen, I should have told you this sooner," Callie said. "I know who Sarrah Sleepz is."

I wasn't surprised—just anxious to get to the truth. "Who is it?"

"Sydney," Callie replied.

I was shocked. "Sydney *Whitman*?"

Callie nodded. My mind was spinning.

"Why? I mean . . . how? She was posting pictures of me in the school hallway. And she's all the way out in California," I said.

"Well, Sydney started the Sarrah Sleepz profile," Callie explained. "She told me and her other friends who she really was. She said she wanted to spy on what was going on at Park Street Middle School without anyone knowing."

"Anyone except you," I said, and Callie looked away.

"It was fun at first," she said. "And then she started commenting on your photos, and it got out of hand, I guess. And when you left PicPop, she asked us to help her, so Olivia took photos of you when you weren't looking."

"You realize how weird that sounds, right?" I asked.

"Well, you don't have to worry about it anymore, because Bella and I told Principal LaCosta it was Sydney," Callie said. "She's calling Sydney's school. And I think anyone from our school who commented is in trouble. Detention, probably. She hasn't decided yet."

"I'm sorry," I said, and then realized how silly it was for me so say that. I didn't have anything to be sorry about. "I mean, thanks for telling the truth to Principal LaCosta."

"It was getting out of hand," Callie repeated, and then she shrugged and walked away.

When I got back to my table, Katie, Alexis, and Emma were practically jumping out of their seats.

"What did she say?" Alexis asked.

I paused dramatically. "Sarrah Sleepz is . . . Sydney Whitman!"

Katie shrieked. Emma gasped.

"I knew it!" Alexis cried.

"You did not," Emma said.

"Well, she was my number one guess. I just

didn't say it out loud, but I had a feeling," Alexis countered.

Katie hugged me. "This means they can stop her, right?"

I nodded. "I think so." And then I repeated what Callie had told me.

"Wow, you really must have made an impression on Sydney for her to bully you from three thousand miles away," Alexis remarked. "It's kind of a compliment."

I had to let that sink in. Alexis was right, in a way. Sydney lived in California. I'd always assumed she would have a glamorous life out there, going to the beach and meeting celebrities and hanging out with popular friends. But if she had nothing better to do than spy on me and make fun of me, maybe things weren't going that well for her.

"I guess you're right," I said. "I'm just glad the whole thing is over!"

CHAPTER 13

When He Looks at Me

$\mathcal{A}$re you really wearing that shirt to the concert?" I asked Dan that night.

We were getting ready to go to the La Vida Pasa concert. I was wearing an official band T-shirt, and skinny jeans. Dan was wearing a scary-looking T-shirt for one of his heavy metal bands. It had a flaming skull on it with snakes coming out of its mouth.

"Why not? It's a music T-shirt," Dan replied.

"We are going to see a Latin pop band, and you are wearing a flaming skull," I told him.

Dan shrugged. "Who cares? Maybe they like flaming skulls."

I thought of the boys in La Vida Pasa, with their button-downed shirts and slouchy jackets. "I don't know about that. It's not exactly the right look."

Sebastian burst through the door. "I'm here! Let's get this party started!"

"You can start the party when you get to the concert," Eddie said, slipping on his jacket. "Everybody ready? Do you have your tickets?"

We all nodded, and then we left the house and piled into Eddie's car. Dan slipped a La Vida Pasa CD into the disc player. Their song, "Lloviendo en mi corazón" came on, which means "Raining in My Heart."

"*Lluvia . . . lluvia . . . lluvia . . . ,*" Sebastian sang along loudly when the chorus came on. "Rain . . . rain . . . rain."

Dan sat in the passenger seat, and he turned around to look at Sebastian.

"Dude, if you sing like that during the concert, I will pretend I don't know you," Dan said.

"Well, I think he sounds nice," I said, partly because it was true and partly to bug Dan.

"Thank you, Mia," Sebastian said, grinning at me.

The Rockwood Arts Center was only forty minutes away from our house in Maple Grove. Eddie dropped us off by the front entrance. We joined the throng of fans, mostly kids and teens,

107

getting through the security checkpoint. I was so excited I could barely stand it.

The guard checked my bag (hairbrush, cell phone, lip gloss). Then we handed in our tickets and entered the ballroom where the concert was being held. It was a big space, with a refreshment stand along one wall and a concert stage all the way along the other.

"I thought there would be seats," I said.

"No seats! This is better. Now, we can dance!" Sebastian began to move to the warm-up music blaring over the speakers.

Dan shook his head. "Dude."

"Hola!"

The sound of three screaming voices behind me made me jump. I turned around and saw, to my amazement, Katie, Alexis, and Emma!

"Oh my!" I cried. "What are you guys doing here?"

"We wanted to surprise you," Katie replied. "I really got into the band after that night you slept over. I kept sharing their videos with Alexis and Emma, and they got into them too."

"We've been practicing our Spanish," Emma said.

"And it's easy to find translations of the songs

online," Alexis added. "So now we at least know what the songs are about."

I stared at my friends, and a feeling of amazing happiness welled up inside me. I couldn't believe they had gone to all that trouble to get to the concert! Then I remembered something.

"So that's why we couldn't bake tonight," I said. "You guys were planning on coming to the concert."

Katie nodded. "Did we surprise you?"

"Yes!" I replied.

"Come on!" Sebastian said, grabbing my hand. "We need to get closer to the front!"

He hurried across the dance floor to the stage, and we followed him. The place was getting more and more packed with each minute. Finally, the recorded music stopped, and the lights dimmed.

A young woman walked out onstage, carrying a guitar.

"Where's the band?" I asked.

"That's the warm-up act," Sebastian explained. "There's always an opening band."

The woman's name was Estela, and she sang really pretty songs in Spanish while she accompanied herself on guitar. I thought she was really good, but I couldn't wait to see La Vida Pasa!

We were watching Estela, swaying to the music, when this guy bumped into me. Really hard.

"Move it!" he said really rudely.

"Um, sorry," I said.

"Yeah, you should be," he retorted, and then I swear he purposely pushed into me again! I started to feel a little scared. What was a guy doing pushing around a middle school girl like me?

Dan, who was standing a little to the side of me, had seen the whole thing and turned to the guy. "You got a problem?" he asked. Dan was about a foot taller than him.

"No, dude, no," the guy said. "Just trying to get to my friend."

I gave Dan a grateful smile. Then it hit me—maybe Mom knew what she was talking about when she made me go to the concert with Dan. Rats! I hate it when parents are right.

By the time Estela finished, the dance floor was so packed that we could barely move. The recorded music came on again for a little while and then stopped when the lights went out. Everyone started to scream—including me!

Then the lights came back on, and Mateo, David, Ian, and Gabriel ran out onto the stage. I started to scream even louder.

They launched into their first song right away. *"Cuando llueve en mi corazón . . ."*

I started singing along, and I noticed that Katie, Emma, and Alexis were singing too! Then Sebastian started to dance, and we all started dancing with him.

Sebastian grabbed Emma's hand and spun her around. I could see her blush. Then he leaned over and said something into her ear.

I couldn't help it—I was curious. I was pretty sure that Emma had a crush on him. Did Sebastian have a crush on her, too?

"What did he say to you?" I shouted in her ear over the music.

"He said, 'Dance with me, my little blond sister,'" she replied.

I looked at her face for a sign of disappointment.

"It's okay," Emma said. "It's good to have a friend."

She didn't look sad at all—maybe because the group had launched into another song—and we started waving our arms and singing along.

I glanced over at Dan. He wasn't dancing, exactly, but he was bobbing his head up and down, and he looked pretty happy.

This is the best night of my life! I thought. They

played almost every song that I loved. And then . . . Mateo pointed out into the crowd.

Katie gasped and nudged me. "He's pointing at you!"

"He is not!" I protested.

But then Mateo spoke into the mic. *"Para la niña con las trenzas!"*

"What did he say?" Katie asked.

I shook my head. "I don't know."

Sebastian turned to us. *"Las trenzas* means 'braids.' That's you, Mia!"

I almost fainted. Mateo smiled, and then they launched into "Cuando ella me mira."

"Wando aya mermaid!" Katie sang along, and I laughed.

"Katie, you know those aren't the words!"

"I know, but I like singing it this way," she replied.

I shook my head, and then I sang along too. And I also changed the words.

"Cuando él me mira!" ("When he looks at me!") Because I would never, ever forget when Mateo looked at me and dedicated the song to the girl with the braids.

Never!

CHAPTER 14

Young and Old

"Are you filling the blueberry cupcakes?" Katie asked Emma.

"No, I'm filling the strawberry cupcakes," Emma replied.

"I'm getting the cream soda cupcakes out of the oven!" Alexis called out.

"I've got the icing the perfect shade of blue," I reported.

It was eleven a.m. in Katie's kitchen, and things were absolutely crazy. We had all the cupcakes baked. The vanilla cupcakes needed their blue and red fillings. The cream soda cupcakes needed to cool. Then everything needed to be iced and decorated.

Katie and Emma filled the vanilla cupcakes

using cupcake plungers. You stick the plunger into the center of a cupcake's top, push the plunger, and a little plug of cake pops out. Then you fill the hole in the cupcake with whatever you want and top it with the cake you just took out.

When the cupcakes were filled, I frosted them all with blue frosting. Then we added the decorations I had prepared: little round red candy-covered chocolates, and little red stars I had cut out of fondant with a tiny cookie cutter.

"Let's do half candies, half stars," I suggested.

"How should we place the red candies?" Alexis asked.

"Maybe place them evenly all over the top, like a checkerboard, almost," I suggested. "And put three stars on each cupcake."

It didn't take long for us to finish the red and blue cupcakes, and we packed them in the special cupcake carriers that we own. By then, the cream soda cupcakes were ready to frost.

"These are going to be delicious," Katie said as she carefully frosted a cupcake with our vanilla cream frosting.

"So, I thought about doing New York City cupcakes," I began to explain. "Taxi cabs, hot dogs, Empire State Building, stuff like that. But to make all that stuff you need a lot of fondant, which isn't supertasty. So this is what I came up with."

I picked up a frosted cupcake, which I sprinkled with gold-colored edible glitter. Finally, I topped it with a cupcake pick with a little flag on top that had a "100" on it in glittery gold numbers.

"I figured that Gladys is turning one hundred, so that's a big deal," I said.

"I love it!" said Alexis. "Did you buy the cupcake picks?"

I shook my head. "I made them myself. I found the glittery numbers in the scrapbook section of the craft store and used them to make the little flags."

"These look awesome," said Katie. "We don't do cupcake picks enough. They're so much fun. I've been looking up some vintage ones online. They're so cute! Little plastic flowers and animals and ballerinas."

"Focus, Katie," Alexis said, looking at the clock. "I'm hoping we'll have time to eat lunch before we head over to the Smiths."

"That's the beauty of the cupcake picks," I said. "It won't take long."

And it didn't. We finished packing the cupcakes and cleaning up by one o'clock, and Katie's mom and her fiancé, Mr. Green (he's a math teacher at our school—long story), surprised us with subs from the deli. I couldn't believe how hungry I was.

"I'm still starving from all that dancing we did last night," Katie said, echoing my feelings.

"Yeah, that was really fun," agreed Emma.

Katie looked for a La Vida Pasa video on her phone and played it, turning up the volume, and we started dancing around the kitchen. Mrs. Brown shook her head.

"I wish I had your energy!" she said.

Pretty soon it was time for us to deliver the cupcakes to the Smiths' party. Alexis's dad has a minivan big enough to hold us, plus eight dozen cupcakes, so he had offered to drive us to our parties.

It was a beautiful fall day, and when we got to the Smiths' house, there were already a bunch of kids running and playing outside. We walked around the house to the backyard, which was decorated with red and blue streamers and balloons.

A woman with long blond hair came up carrying a little blond boy.

"Hi, Alexis," she said. "This must be the Cupcake Club. This is Evan. It's his birthday today."

Evan smiled at us with the cutest smile in the whole world.

"Happy birthday!" we all told Evan.

Two little blond-haired girls ran up.

"Mom! Mom! Daddy's setting up the basketball pole!" said one of the girls.

"I want him to set up the craft table now!" said the other.

"Calm down, girls," Mrs. Smith said. "Everything will get set up soon. Right now, I've got to set up these cupcakes."

"We'll do that for you," Emma said quickly. "You've got your hands full."

Mrs. Smith smiled gratefully. "Thanks! They go on that table over there."

She motioned to a small round table set up with a red tablecloth.

"Oh, this is going to be perfect!" I said.

We had brought red and blue cupcake stands, and I set those up on the table. Then we carefully set up four dozen blue and red cupcakes on the stands. I stood back to admire it when we were done.

"Perfect!" I said. "Looks very superhero-y."

Evan came running toward the cupcake table, chased by his screaming sisters. Emma scooped him up before he could knock into the table. His mom came running up.

"Thanks," she said, then noticed the table. "Wow,

these look fantastic! Thanks so much, girls. Let me get my checkbook."

Mrs. Smith paid us, and we headed back to the Becker minivan to our next destination. As I walked through the backyard, I noticed all the party activities. A short basketball pole with a foam basketball. A craft table with coloring books and sticker books. Lots of toy trucks and cars.

I remembered my first birthday parties in New York City. We never had them in the apartment. Mom and Dad would rent out a room in a pizza place or an ice-cream shop. There were always silly games to play, and we would make jewelry or color pictures. It wasn't that long ago, really, but it seemed like forever. Those parties were fun, I realized, but I've definitely outgrown them.

"Next stop, Maple Grove Senior Home!" Mr. Becker announced as we climbed back into the minivan.

The atmosphere at the Maple Grove home was very different from the Smith's backyard. We walked through the entrance into a bright, wide lobby. There were some elderly people sitting in chairs, and some in wheelchairs, and it was very quiet.

Alexis told the woman at the front desk that we

were here with the cupcakes, and a minute later, another woman came to the desk to greet us.

"Holly Greenberg," she said, pumping Alexis's hand up and down. "Thanks for bringing the cupcakes. Everyone is so excited for the party."

I looked around at the people in the lobby. Except for the two people playing checkers, everyone else looked like they were napping. I glanced at Katie.

"Wait until you meet Gladys," she said.

Holly led us to the dining room, which had been decorated for the birthday party. A big banner reading HAPPY 100 was hanging across the wall. Holly instructed us to set up the cupcakes on a table at the end of the room.

"Let me go get Gladys," Holly said. "She'll want to thank you."

Holly left and returned a few minutes later with a tiny woman on her arm. Gladys had the prettiest snow-white hair I had ever seen, and bright blue eyes that peered through wire-rimmed glasses. She smiled when she saw us.

"Katie, these must be the friends you were telling us about," Gladys said.

"Yes, this is Alexis, Emma, and Mia," responded Katie, pointing to each of us.

"Let me see those beautiful cupcakes," Gladys said, and she walked toward the table. "Look at that glitter! I love it. What flavor are they?"

"It's a surprise flavor," Katie told her. "We made you cream soda cupcakes."

Gladys's eyes got wide. "Cream soda cupcakes? I have lived one hundred years, and I've never heard of such a thing. They sound delicious." She reached for one.

"Gladys, those are for dessert later," Holly scolded her.

"Oh, pooh! It's my birthday," Gladys said, and she unwrapped the cupcake and bit into it. Then she made what I call the "cupcake face." That's the face people make when they really love our cupcakes. Mainly, they close their eyes.

Gladys's eyes were closed for what felt like a long time. Then she opened them. "It tastes just like cream soda. Delicious!"

Alexis approached her. "Mrs. Bailey, I have a question for you. What advice do you have for living to one hundred?"

Katie and Gladys both laughed, and Alexis looked confused.

"I told her you were going to ask that!" Katie said.

"And I've been thinking about the answer," Gladys replied. "I would have to say, take a walk every day. And a nap. But mostly, do what you love with people you love."

Emma started tearing up. "That's beautiful."

Katie hugged Gladys. "Happy birthday," she said. "Have a good party!"

"Oh, I'm sure I will," Gladys replied. "My grandchildren will be here. We're going to play Scrabble."

"They'll be here soon, so you should get ready," Holly told her. Then she turned to us. "The cupcakes are beautiful. You girls are really professional."

"Thank you," Alexis said, shaking her hand. Alexis was beaming. I know that's her favorite compliment.

We walked back outside.

"No basketball hoop at this party," Katie joked.

"No, but Scrabble is fun," Alexis said.

"Not as fun as last night," Emma pointed out.

I had to agree. And then I realized something. I was too old for some things. And too young for other things. But I was still having a good time.

"I feel like we should do something," I said when we got back into the car. "Does anybody want to go to the mall, maybe?"

"I'm happy to drive you there," Mr. Becker said.

"Just as long as it's okay with everyone's parents."

Emma, Katie, and I started texting furiously. (It was good to have my phone back.) A few minutes later I was walking through the mall with my friends, talking and laughing.

I was doing what I loved with people I loved, just like Gladys had said. Who knows? Maybe I'll live to one hundred. But if I do, I hope I'll be dancing on my birthday instead of playing Scrabble!

Want a BONUS cupcake?
Here's a small taste
of the very first book in the

CUPCAKE DIARIES

series:

Katie
and the
cupcake cure

Who's Afraid of Middle School? Not Me!

*E*very time I have ever watched a movie about middle school, the main character is always freaking out before the first day of school. You know what I mean, right? If the movie's about a guy, he's always worried about getting stuffed into a garbage can by jocks. If it's about a girl, she's trying on a zillion outfits and screaming when she sees a pimple on her face. And no matter what movie it is, the main character is always obsessed with being popular.

My name is Katie Brown, and whenever I watched those movies, I just didn't get it. I mean, how could middle school be *that* different from elementary school? Yeah, I knew there would be new kids from other schools, but I figured everyone from our school would stick together. We've all pretty much known one another since kinder-garten. Sure, not everybody hangs out together, but it's not like we put some kids on a pedestal and worship them or anything. We're all the same. Back in third grade, we all got sick together on mystery meat loaf day. That kind of experience has to bind you for life, doesn't it?

That's what I thought, anyway. I didn't spend one single second of the summer worrying about middle school. I got a really bad sunburn at the town pool, made a thousand friendship bracelets at day camp, and learned from my mom how to make a cake that looks like an American flag. I didn't stress out about middle school at all.

Guess what? I was wrong! But you probably knew that already. Yeah, the cruel hammer of reality hit pretty hard on the very first day of school. And the worst thing was, I wasn't even expecting it.

The morning started out normal. I put on the tie-dyed T-shirt I made at day camp, my favorite pair of jeans, and a new pair of white sneakers. Then I slipped about ten friendship bracelets on each arm, which I thought looked pretty cool. I brushed my hair, which takes about thirty seconds. My hair is brown and wavy—Mom calls it au naturel. I only worry about my hair when it starts to hang in my eyes, and then I cut it.

When I went downstairs for breakfast, Mom was waiting for me in the kitchen.

"Happy first day of middle school, Katie!" she shouted.

Did I mention that my mom is supercorny? I think it's because she's a dentist. I read a survey once that said that people are afraid of dentists more than anything else, even zombies and funeral directors. (Which is totally not fair, because without dentists everybody would have rotten teeth, and without teeth you can't eat corn on the cob, which is delicious.) But anyway, I think she tries to smile all the time and make jokes so that people will like her more. Not that she's fake—she's honestly pretty nice, for a mom.

"I made you a special breakfast," Mom told me. "A banana pancake shaped like a school bus!"

The pancake sat on a big white plate. Mom had used banana slices for wheels and square pieces of cantaloupe for the windows. This might seem like a strange breakfast to you, but my mom does stuff like this all the time. She wanted to go to cooking school when she got out of high school, but her parents wanted her to be a dentist, like them. Which is unfair, except that if she didn't go to dental school, she wouldn't have met my dad, and I would never have been born, so I guess I can't complain.

But anyway, in her free time she does the whole Martha Stewart thing. Not that she looks like Martha Stewart. She has brown hair like me, but hers is curly, and her favorite wardrobe items are her blue dentist coat and her apron that says #1 CHEF on the front. This morning she was wearing both.

"Thanks, Mom," I said. I didn't say anything about being too old for a pancake shaped like a school bus. It would have hurt her feelings. Besides, it was delicious.

She sat down in the seat next to me and sipped her coffee. "Do you have the map I printed out for you with the new bus stop location?" she asked me. She was doing that biting-her-bottom-lip thing she does when she's worried about me, which is most of the time.

"I got it, but I don't need it," I replied. "It's only four blocks away."

Mom frowned. "Okay. But I e-mailed the map to Barbara just in case."

Barbara is my mom's best friend—and she's also the mom of my own best friend, Callie. We've known each other since we were babies. Callie is two months older than I am, and she never lets me forget it.

"I hope Callie has the map," my mom went on. "I wouldn't want you two to get lost on your first day of middle school."

"We won't," I promised. "I'm meeting Callie at the corner of Ridge Street, and we're walking to the bus stop together."

"Oh, good," Mom said. "I'm glad you finally talked to your old bus buddy."

"Uh, yeah," I said, and quickly gulped down some orange juice. I hadn't actually talked to her. But we'd been bus buddies ever since kindergarten (my corny mom came up with "bus buddies," in case you didn't figure that out already), so there was no real reason to believe this year would be any different. I knew I'd see her at the bus stop.

Every August, Callie goes to sleepaway camp, which totally stinks. She doesn't get back until a few days before school starts. Normally I see her the first day she comes back and we go to King Cone for ice cream.

But this year Callie texted that she was busy shopping with her mom. Callie has always cared a lot more about clothes than I do. She wanted to find the perfect outfit to wear on her first day of middle school. And since we only had a few days before school started I didn't think it was *that* weird that I didn't see her. It was a *little* weird that she hadn't called me back. But we had texted and agreed to meet on the corner of Ridge Street, so I was sure everything was fine.

I ate my last bite of pancake and stood up. "Gotta brush my teeth," I said. When you're the daughter of a dentist, you get into that habit pretty early.

Soon I was slipping on my backpack and heading for the door. Of course, Mom grabbed me and gave me a big hug.

"I packed you a special lunch, Cupcake," she said.

Mom has called me Cupcake ever since I can remember. I kind of like it—except when she says it in front of other people.

"A special lunch? Really?" I teased her. Every lunch she makes me is a special lunch. "What a surprise."

"I love you!" Mom called. I turned and waved. For a second I thought she was going to follow me to the bus so I yelled, "I love you too!" and ran down the driveway.

Outside, it still felt like summer. *I should have worn shorts,* I thought. There's nothing worse than sitting in a hot classroom sweating a lot and having your jeans stick to your legs. Gross. But it was too late to change now.

Ridge Street was only two blocks away. There were lots of kids heading for the bus stop, but I didn't see Callie. I stood on the corner, tapping my foot.

"Come on, Callie," I muttered. If we missed the bus, Mom would insist on walking me to the bus stop every morning. I didn't know if I could take that much cheerfulness before seven thirty a.m.

Then a group of girls turned the corner: Sydney Whitman, Maggie Rodriguez, and Brenda Kovacs—and Callie was with them! I was a little confused. Callie usually didn't walk with them. It was always just Callie and me.

"Hey, Cal!" I called out.

Callie looked up at me and waved, but continued talking to Maggie.

That was strange. I noticed, though, she wasn't wearing her glasses. She's as blind as a bat without her glasses. *Maybe she doesn't recognize me,* I reasoned. *My hair did get longer this summer.*

So I ran up to them. That's when I noticed they were all dressed kind of alike—even Callie. They were wearing skinny jeans and each girl had on a different color T-shirt and a thick belt.

"Hey, guys," I said. "The bus stop's this way." I nodded toward Ridge Street.

Callie looked at me and smiled. "Hi, Katie! We were just talking about walking to school," she said.

"Isn't it kind of far to walk?" I asked.

Maggie spoke up. "Only little kids take the bus."

"Oh," I said. (I know, I sound like a genius. But I was thinking about how my mom probably wouldn't like the idea of us walking to school.)

Then Sydney looked me up and down. "Nice shirt, Katie," she said. But she said it in a way that I knew meant she definitely didn't think it was nice. "Did you make that at camp?"

Maggie and Brenda giggled.

"As a matter of fact, I did," I said.

I looked at Callie. I didn't say anything. She didn't say anything. What was going on?

"Come on," Sydney said, linking arms with Callie. "I don't want to be late."

She didn't say, "Come on, everybody but Katie," but she might as well have. I knew I wasn't invited. Callie turned around and waved. "See you later!" she called.

I stood there, frozen, as my best friend walked away from me like I was some kind of stranger.

The Horrible Truth Hits Me

You might think I was mad at Callie. But I wasn't. Well, not really. For the most part I was really confused.

Why didn't Callie ask me to walk with them? Something had to be going on. Like, maybe her mom had told her to walk with those girls for some reason. Or maybe Callie didn't ask me to walk with them because she figured I would be the one to ask. Maybe that was it.

The sound of a bus engine interrupted my thoughts. Two blocks away, I could see a yellow school bus turning the corner. I was going to miss it!

I tore off down the sidewalk. It's a good thing I'm a fast runner because I got to the bus stop just as the last kid was getting on board. I climbed up the steps, and the bus driver gave me a nod. She was a friendly-looking woman with a round face and curly black hair.

It hit me for the first time that I would have a new bus driver now that I was going to middle school. The elementary school bus driver, Mr. Hopkins, was really nice. And I might never see him again!

But I couldn't think about that now. I had to find a place to sit. Callie and I always sat in the third seat down on the right. Two boys I didn't know were sitting in that seat. I stood there, staring at the seats, not knowing what to do.

"Please find a seat," the bus driver told me.

I walked down the aisle. Maybe there was something in the back. As I passed the sixth row, a girl nodded to the empty seat next to her. I quickly slid into it, and the bus lurched forward.

"Thanks," I said.

"No problem," replied the girl. "I'm Mia."

I don't really know a lot about fashion, but I could tell that Mia was wearing stuff that you see in magazines. She could even have been a model herself—she had long black hair that wasn't dull like mine, but shiny and bouncy. She was wearing those leggings that look like jeans, with black boots, and a short black jacket over a long gray T-shirt. I figured that Mia must be a popular girl from one of the other elementary schools.

"Are you from Richardson?" I asked her. "I used to go to Hamilton."

Mia shook her head. "I just moved here a few weeks ago. From Manhattan."

"Mia from Manhattan. That's easy to remember," I said. I started talking a mile a minute, like I do when I'm nervous or excited. "I never met anyone who lived in Manhattan before. I've only been there once. We saw *The Lion King* on Broadway. I just remember it was really crowded and really noisy. Was it noisy where you lived?"

"My neighborhood was pretty quiet," Mia replied.

I suddenly realized that my question might have been insulting.

"Not that noisy is bad," I said quickly. "I just meant—you know, the cars and buses and people and stuff . . ." I decided I wasn't making things any better.

But Mia didn't seem to mind. "You're right. It can get pretty crazy. But I like it there," she said. "I still live there, kind of. My dad does, anyway."

Were her parents divorced like mine? I wondered.

I wanted to ask her, but it seemed like a really personal question. I chose a safer subject. "So, how do you like Maple Grove?"

"It's pretty here," she answered. "It's just kind of … quiet."

She smiled, and I smiled back. "Yeah, things can be pretty boring around here," I said.

"By the way, I like your shirt," Mia told me. "Did you make it yourself?"

I got a sick feeling for a second—was she making fun of me, like Sydney had? But the look on her face told me she was serious.

"Thanks," I said, relieved. "I'm glad you said that because somebody earlier didn't like it at all, and what was extra weird is that my best friend was hanging around with that person."

"That sounds complicated," Mia said.

That's when the bus pulled into the big round driveway in front of Park Street Middle School. I'd seen the school a million times before, of course, since it was right off the main road. And I'd been inside once, last June, when the older kids had given us a tour. I just remember thinking how much bigger it was than my elementary school. The guide leading us kept saying it was shaped like a *U* so it was easy to get around. But it didn't seem easy to me.

We climbed out of the bus, which had stopped in front of the wide white steps that led up to the front door. The concrete building was the color of beach sand, and for a second I wished it was still summer and I was back on the beach.

Mia took a piece of yellow paper out of her jacket pocket. "My homeroom is in room 212," she said. "What's yours?"

I shrugged off my backpack. My schedule was somewhere inside. I zipped it open and started searching through my folders.

"I've got to find mine," I said. "Go on ahead."

"Are you sure?" Mia looked hesitant. If I hadn't been freaking out about my schedule, I might have noticed that she didn't want to go in alone. But I wasn't thinking too clearly.

"Yeah," I said. "I'll see you later!"

After what seemed forever I finally found my schedule tucked inside one of the pockets of my five-subject notebook. I looked on the line that read HOMEROOM . . . 216.

So I wouldn't be with Mia. But would I be with Callie? She and I had meant to go over our schedules to see what classes we'd have together. Now I didn't know if we had the same gym or lunch or anything.

Maybe we're in the same homeroom, I thought hopefully. I studied the little map on the bottom of the schedule and went inside. From the front door, it was pretty easy to find room 216. It looked like a social studies classroom, I guessed. There were maps of the world on the wall and a big globe in the corner. I scanned the room for Callie, but I didn't see her, although Maggie and Brenda were there, sitting next to each other. Almost all of the seats were taken; the only empty ones were in the front row, where nobody ever wants to sit. But I had no choice.

I purposely took the seat in front of Maggie— partly because I knew her from my old school, and partly because I wanted to get some info about Callie.

I set my backpack on the floor and turned around. Maggie and Brenda were drawing with gel pens on their notebooks. They were both tracing the letters "PGC" in big bubble print. When they saw me looking, they quickly flipped over their notebooks.

"Hey," I said. "Do you know if Callie is in this homeroom?"

"Why don't you ask her yourself?" Maggie asked, and Brenda burst out into giggles.

"Um, okay," I said, but I could feel my face getting red. Callie and I had never hung out with Sydney, Maggie, and Brenda at our old school, but they had always been basically nice. At least, they'd never been mean to me.

But I guess things had changed.

The bell rang, and for the first time, I felt a pang of middle school fear. Just like those kids in the movies.

It was a horrible thought, but I knew it was true.... Middle school wasn't going to be as easy as I'd hoped!

Want more

CUPCAKE DIARIES?

Visit **CupcakeDiariesBooks.com**
for the series trailer, excerpts, activities,
and everything you need for throwing
your own cupcake party!

Still Hungry?
There's always room for another Cupcake!

Katie and the cupcake cure

CUPCAKE DIARIES

by coco simon

Mia in the mix

CUPCAKE DIARIES

by coco simon

Emma on thin icing

CUPCAKE DIARIES

by coco simon

Alexis and the perfect recipe

CUPCAKE DIARIES

by coco simon

Katie, batter up!

CUPCAKE DIARIES

by coco simon

Mia's baker's dozen

CUPCAKE DIARIES

by coco simon

CUPCAKE DIARIES
Emma
all stirred up!
by coco simon

CUPCAKE DIARIES
Alexis
cool as a cupcake
by coco simon

CUPCAKE DIARIES
Katie
and the cupcake war
by coco simon

CUPCAKE DIARIES
Mia's
boiling point
by coco simon

CUPCAKE DIARIES
Emma,
smile and say "cupcake!"
by coco simon

CUPCAKE DIARIES
Alexis
gets frosted
by coco simon

CUPCAKE DIARIES
Katie's
new recipe
by coco simon

CUPCAKE DIARIES
Mia
a matter of taste
by coco simon

CUPCAKE DIARIES
Emma
sugar and spice and everything nice
by coco simon

CUPCAKE DIARIES
Alexis
and the missing ingredient
by coco simon

CUPCAKE DIARIES
Katie
sprinkles & surprises
by coco simon

CUPCAKE DIARIES
Mia
fashion plates and cupcakes
by coco simon

Coco Simon always dreamed of opening a cupcake bakery but was afraid she would eat all of the profits. When she's not daydreaming about cupcakes, Coco edits children's books and has written close to one hundred books for children, tweens, and young adults, which is a lot less than the number of cupcakes she's eaten. Cupcake Diaries is the first time Coco has mixed her love of cupcakes with writing.

If you liked

CUPCAKE  DIARIES

be sure to check out these

other series from

Simon Spotlight

IT TAKES TWO

If you like reading about the adventures of Katie, Mia, Emma, and Alexis, you'll love Alex and Ava, stars of the It Takes Two series!

sewzoey

Zoey's clothing design blog puts her on the A-list in the fashion world . . . but when it comes to school, will she be teased, or will she be a trendsetter? Find out in the Sew Zoey series:

Did you LOVE reading this book?

Visit the Whyville...

Where you can:

- ⬡ Discover great books!
- ⬡ Meet new friends!
- ⬡ Read exclusive sneak peeks and more!

Log on to visit now!
bookhive.whyville.net

Looking for another great book?
Find it
IN THE MIDDLE.

Fun, fantastic books for kids
in the in-beTWEEN age.

IntheMiddleBooks.com

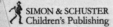